Adam Fitzroy

Dear Mister President

Manifold Press

Published by Manifold Press

ISBN: 978-1-908312-82-2

Proof-reading and line editing: Thalia Communications | thaliacomm.net

Editor: Fiona Pickles

For further details of Manifold Press titles both in print and forthcoming: manifoldpress.co.uk

Other titles by Adam Fitzroy:
    Between Now and Then
    The Bridge on the River Wye
    Ghost Station
    Make Do and Mend
    Stage Whispers

Acknowledgements

The author wishes to thank:
Marilyn, Louise, Chris,
Tray, Alayne, Marian
and everyone else who kindly
read the manuscript and
offered suggestions and amendments.

1.

"At ease there, son, and take a load off."

The man who spoke was bulky, gray-haired and smiling. He was dressed in outrageous plaid pants and an open-necked shirt as if he had just arrived post-haste from the golf course – which would not have been an unreasonable place to be on a warm Spring Saturday afternoon – and breezed into the highly secure Pennsylvania Avenue office as if he owned it. As indeed, for the duration of the current administration, he did. Big and folksy and pushing seventy, Mitchell Booth took up a considerable amount of space although he was scarcely more than five-foot ten; it was his personality that dominated the room, however, rather than his physique, expanding to fill its unvisited recesses, setting the air thrumming with the insistent vibration of far-off heavy machinery.

"Thank you, sir."

Colonel Charles Chadwick Ryan – a quarter century younger and several inches shorter – shook the starch out of his shoulders, folded himself into the chair indicated and took advantage of this first real opportunity to assess his surroundings. The room was comfortable bordering on plush, every item of furniture as well as the garden view of manicured green not merely suggesting but rather shouting aloud that here was the abode of a man who had made it to the top of his profession and was set on enjoying whatever perks came with the job. For that guileless determination, Ryan could hardly find it in his heart to criticize him.

"I've got some coffee coming," Booth said, looking round as an attractive young woman entered and set down a tray. "Thank you."

The girl did not glance at either of them. She merely checked the tray and left again, closing the door behind her, and as soon as she had gone Booth strode to the chair opposite Ryan and poured coffee for himself as well as for his guest.

"I understand you're making a good recovery from your injuries?" he remarked.

Ryan's mouth twitched at the bluntness of the question. In the past six months, a lot of people had wanted to talk to him about what would go down in history as a foiled Presidential assassination attempt; some had approached it subtly and some had not. News and media outlets had been relentless in pursuing him, hailing him as 'The Quiet Hero', using expressions that often included the words 'conscientious' and 'unassuming' as if they could find nothing interesting to say about someone essentially so colorless. He had been a week or two's sensation, that was all; the USAF officer who had thrown himself between a President and an armed man and had taken two bullets that shattered his shoulder into a dozen fragments. Then the news cycle had moved on and left him, mercifully, to his own devices; football players and reality TV stars took over the headlines, wars were declared in countries nobody had ever heard of, blockbuster movies were released, and he just wasn't important any more. To suggest that he had greeted this development with profound relief would have been an understatement.

"Yes, sir, thank you. I'm told I'll be fit to return to work in the next couple of weeks."

"Uh-huh." Booth absorbed the information without troubling to conceal that he knew it already. "What then? Keen to go back to your old posting? Or would you prefer a different challenge?"

Ryan, who had been in the act of reaching for a cup, let his hand drop and sat back in his chair again for a moment. When he had been informed – to his astonishment – that he was required to meet with the National Security Advisor at the White House, one of many scenarios to have wandered through his mind was the possibility that he might be offered a job. He had dismissed it on the grounds of his present position being too lowly and his service background too specialized for him to be of use in any other capacity. Image interpretation, even given the sophisticated techniques of which he was master, was not likely to be in particular demand among the President's staff. They could have found a dozen men better qualified than himself – as well as younger – for any vacant post they might happen to have available.

"I haven't thought about it, sir," he said. "I took it for granted I'd be going back to my old job."

"But you wouldn't be opposed to the possibility of a change?"

Feeling steadier, Ryan reached again for the coffee cup. "Not in principle. It would depend on the nature of the opportunity."

"Wise man. Well, let me lay it on the line for you. My Deputy, Ted Flanagan, is being retired on health grounds. He went for a physical the week before last and the doctors say his arteries are so clogged they're barely viable. They're talking about bypass surgery and I don't know what the hell else; months of recovery. He took the weekend to talk it over with his wife and kids, then came back and said he wanted to retire – some damned thing about a farm in Oklahoma and breeding horses; I tuned out, it was like an episode of *The Waltons*. Anyway, this'll be a short-term posting unless we're re-elected – and at the moment that's not looking likely. So, how about it? Are you interested?"

Startled, Ryan could not at first form a coherent reply. "I'm flattered," he said, "but I don't understand … I mean, I don't know what I'd have to offer at this level. I'm not sure I have any relevant experience."

Booth grunted. "Well," he said, "I've seen your file, so let's not pretend you're not adequately qualified. I notice you're not married," he went on. "Why is that? In my experience, a wife is usually considered an asset for a military man."

Ryan's eyebrows lifted. "Usual reason, sir."

"Too busy working on your career?"

"No, sir. I'm gay."

The only response from across the room was a slow nodding of the head. "Okay," Booth said, without hostility. "Feel good to say it out loud? Spent too long having to hide it?"

"Pretty much. The *'Don't ask, Don't tell'* thing was a nightmare."

"Well, I'm sure you realize it won't make an atom of difference around here," Booth told him. "This administration celebrates diversity."

"Yes, sir. The President's views are well known – although I'm hoping this isn't some kind of affirmative-action appointment?"

"Sure it is. It's part of the President's drive to recruit Air Force officers named Ryan who've saved his life recently; he considers them a neglected minority. Got a partner? Anyone we need to make background checks on?"

"No, sir." Ryan let the matter drop. "My last relationship was some years ago. I don't ... " A tactful pause, then; "I don't visit clubs or engage in casual sex."

"I hope you don't actually hate women?"

"No, sir, not at all. Why would you ask?"

Booth chuckled easily, not remotely disconcerted by the subject. "There'll be times when you'll be attached to the First Lady's escort team. I just wanted to make sure that wouldn't be uncomfortable for either of you."

"Sir, I'd be proud to escort the First Lady at any time."

"Good. I think she'd like you, you seem to have a similar sense of humor. You do understand, don't you, that being seen in public with the First Family could attract attention towards you just when things are starting to settle down a bit? I have to tell you, your present CO is concerned about that. He says you're a back-room boy at heart and you'd rather be doing something behind the scenes than standing in the limelight taking the applause. Would you consider that a fair summation?"

"Yes, sir, I would."

"Okay. The problem with that, Charles ... Is it Charles? Charlie? Chuck?"

"Charles is fine. Or Chad."

"Chad. Hmmm." Booth evaluated the name. "Yeah, I like that. The problem with that, Chad," he resumed, not missing a beat, "is that for a man who wanted to keep a low profile, you made a big mistake. Saving the President's life is the kind of thing that's liable to get you noticed."

Ryan glanced away. It was always uncomfortable to hear himself praised, even indirectly, for something he hadn't considered extraordinary. As a serving officer, his life was at the disposal of his Commander-in-Chief; it was as simple as that.

"Sir," he said at last, "may I speak frankly?"

Booth laughed. "You'd better, or I may have to withdraw my offer."

"Yes sir. As a matter of fact ... I don't think I did save his life. I mean, in my opinion the Secret Service over-reacted. I'm certain Captain Corrado had no intention of harming the President."

"He was waving a firearm around within fifty feet of him," was the sharp reminder. "In an area that had supposedly been secured. That made him a legitimate threat. You know they can't afford to take any chances. And I might also point out you that you jumped in to stop him."

"Only because I was trying to prevent exactly what happened. Corrado needed psychiatric help, not a bullet. In fact, from what I've heard since, it seems as if he'd needed it for a long time. He was more messed up than anybody ever realized, and the extra pressure of the President's visit pushed him over the edge. He was a loyal man, sir; he couldn't possibly have understood what he was doing. I don't want him made the scapegoat for other people's failings now that he isn't around to defend himself. Somebody should be stating his point of view, sir," Ryan concluded abruptly, "and it might as well be me."

He stopped, certain he had over-stepped the mark and probably effectively sabotaged his own chances. Booth, however, was nodding thoughtfully.

"Believe it or not, that's almost exactly what the President says. But you both know the Secret Service never gives anybody the benefit of the doubt. They lost Kennedy, they nearly lost Reagan, they don't want it to happen again; it's a matter of pride. Besides, this is supposed to be a democracy; there are ways of expressing your opinion that don't involve pointing a gun at anybody."

"Yes, sir, I know. But a man with severe mental affliction is not capable of rational decisions. There should be room for clemency in a case like that."

"There wasn't time." Booth sounded weary, as if he'd said these words too many times before. "We all wish it hadn't happened, Chad, the President most of all, but when I look back on it now I wouldn't want the Secret Service to have acted any differently than they did. When they're protecting my President, I want them to be ruthless. I don't want them to think twice about whether or not they're doing the right thing. What I do want, on the other hand, is for them to be absolutely certain an area is clear before they allow the President into it; that doesn't seem a lot to ask, does it?"

"No, sir, it doesn't."

"They're going to have to do better in future. Mistakes were made. But progress is a steamroller, and sometimes people get crushed who shouldn't be. Captain Corrado was one of those people."

"I'd be sorry to think so, sir."

"Well, so would I, but unfortunately it's too late to do anything about it now except learn the lesson."

"Yes."

A discontented silence fell. There was plenty that was still unpalatable about the circumstances of the incident, and would always remain so; without question it should not have been left to one Air Force officer, marginally more alert than anybody else in the room, to interpose himself between the putative assassin and the target; the occasion should not have arisen in the first place.

"I'm assuming, then," Booth said, after a moment of consideration, "that you feel our positions on the matter are too far apart for us to work together?"

"No, sir." Then, recollecting himself sharply, Ryan continued; "I mean, no, sir, that isn't what I think. It's probably not the only subject we'll disagree on and if you ask for my opinion that's what you'll get. On the other hand, if you don't ask I won't volunteer it."

"So you're accepting the job, then? Not going to ask about pay, hours, duties?"

"No, sir. You won't pay less than I'm earning at the moment and long hours don't concern me. As for duties, if you think I'm the man for the job then whatever you give me to do, I'll do."

Booth grimaced. "Careful what you promise," he warned. "The duties in this case are what you might call 'flexible'. Ted Flanagan wasn't so much a Deputy NSA as a buddy and there's going to be a Flanagan-sized hole in the President's life from now on. He'll need somebody to kick back and watch a movie with, just as much as somebody to advise on Iraqi troop movements. You may end up being more of a baby-sitter than a bodyguard. How would you feel about that?"

"More importantly, sir, how would the President feel about it? If he's had the Colonel around for such a long time, how's he going to respond to having someone he doesn't know suddenly in his place?"

"Well, any decision you and I make is subject to his approval, but I can tell you that approaching you was his idea. He saw you being interviewed on television and said we should have a conversation. He said any guy capable of being that charming but still saying absolutely nothing was the kind of person he wanted to have around. And giving you a job in the White House after what you did wouldn't be the worst move in the world from a publicity point of view, either. But you know Doug Kearney, he'd rather do the right thing that the popular one, which is why at the moment his approval rating's somewhere in the basement."

There did not seem much to be said in response to this, so Ryan remained silent. It was only seconds, however, before Booth began speaking again.

"You like him?"

"Sir?"

"The President. Did you vote for him?"

"Oh. Yes, sir, I did, as a matter of fact. I'm very much in favor of some of his primary policy initiatives."

"Well, good, that's a start. How about as an individual? You think you'd get along? Only this job is going to involve you spending a lot of time with him – and some of that will be alone."

"I don't know much about him personally, sir, except that he's smarter than the average President and he seems to care about his family. If I had a criticism, I'd say he's spreading himself a little too thin; he always looks tired."

"You're right there," Booth told him. "But I never met a President yet who didn't try to do it all in his first couple of years; they're planning for the legacy almost before they park their backsides behind the *Resolute* desk. There's never enough time."

"No, sir."

"Okay. Any plans for this evening?"

The sudden change of subject was almost enough to knock Ryan out of his stride, but he took a deep breath and replied as calmly as if he had noticed nothing.

"Microwave dinner for one and catching up on laundry," he suggested, with wry embarrassment.

"Demanding social life, huh? Well, maybe you could postpone. I'd like you to come upstairs and meet the President; if he signs off on your appointment, you can come back Monday morning and expect to work harder than you've ever worked in your life. Deal?"

"Yes, sir, it's a deal."

"Okay. And, for the record, when you're out of uniform, you're going to be calling me 'Mitch' like everybody else."

The thought was far from comfortable, but it was so much less intimidating than the prospect of actually meeting the President that Ryan merely nodded.

"Uhm, okay," he said. "Sir."

"You'll get used to it. Now, if you're ready," Booth went on, "we can go out this way and up a staircase at the end; this is the way you'll go when the President's in the Oval Office. Well, there's lots of stuff like that – things you need to be aware of. I'll make sure you're fully briefed on Monday."

"Thank you, sir." Ryan noticed that any possibility of his being unsuitable for the job appeared to have been discarded, at least for the time being. Mitchell Booth certainly seemed to consider it a done deal.

"One more thing. Everybody in this building has enemies, and yours are lining up against you already. They're powerful people who can do you a lot of damage if they want to – you'll soon find out who they are. Whatever happens, don't try to involve the President in any kind of personal rivalry between yourself and another member of staff. Understood?"

"Understood," Ryan told him, following him through a paneled door and into a quiet corridor outside.

They moved quickly up a narrow staircase guarded by a smart-suited agent who nodded at Booth as they passed, along a corridor with a couple of bewildering twists and past two further sets of Secret Service personnel until they stopped at a plain white door in a quiet dead-end at the rear of the building. Booth knocked, but without waiting for a reply immediately opened the door and stepped inside.

"Mr President? I'd like you to meet Colonel Chad Ryan."

On the far side of what appeared to be a comfortable, even chaotic, private sitting room, a figure unfolded itself from a disreputable old couch and advanced towards them. Douglas Ford Kearney, fifty-six years of age, who had risen to the White House from political obscurity as the junior Senator for Vermont, was a tall and vigorous man with brown hair beginning to be flecked with gray. He had compelling hazel eyes and the firm mouth and stubborn jawline of a man accustomed to having his own way. He held out a hand by way of greeting.

"I think we've met before," he said. "Under less congenial circumstances."

"Yes, Mr President. Good evening." Ryan accepted the handshake almost casually, surprised by Kearney's evident awkwardness and unaccustomed air of vulnerability. It was not a shock, however, that the grip seemed slightly prolonged and firmer than formality demanded; the welcome, although low-key, could hardly have been warmer.

"I'm sorry I couldn't get to the hospital; my security people were against it."

"I understand, sir. I was grateful for your letter."

Kearney's mouth twisted in disapproval. "That was one of those formal things," he said, uneasily. "You know, where you release the text to the media. I figured I'd wait and thank you properly when we met in person. You want to hang out for an hour or so and get a beer and a sandwich with me?"

"Do I ... ?"

"I make sure I get an evening off from time to time," Kearney explained. "I like to watch football or a movie and pretend I'm a normal guy. When my wife and daughter are in town, this is their room, but they let me use it sometimes."

"Yes sir."

"Is that 'yes sir' to the beer and the sandwich, Colonel?" Kearney asked, one graying eyebrow lifting mischievously.

"Yes, sir, it is."

"Good." The President slapped him on the arm and then glanced over his shoulder. "How about you, Mitch? Are you joining us?"

"I wish I could, Mr President, but Jeannie's got a whole load of people coming over for dinner, so if you don't need me I ought to be getting back."

"Sure, you go ahead. I'll see you in the morning."

"Thank you sir. Have a good evening." And, just as if he were a neighbor calling by to return a borrowed lawnmower and seeing no reason to turn it into a social occasion, Mitchell Booth disappeared back around the door and left the two men alone together in the room.

"He's a good man," Kearney observed, absently. "We've known each other since dinosaurs ruled the Earth." Then he seemed to recollect his duties as the host and continued. "The sandwiches should be here soon and there's beer in the fridge. Take your jacket off, loosen your tie, pick out a movie; everything in that pile on the table is something I haven't seen before."

There was a hollowness behind the words, however, as though Kearney was just repeating what he knew to be correct without having any real concept of what it meant. He might as well have been speaking Mandarin.

Self-consciously Ryan discarded his jacket, draping it over the back of a small chair, and hauled his tie low enough to unfasten the top button of his shirt. The President was in the remnant of a business suit, shirt open at the collar, tie askew, sleeves rolled. He had long ago abandoned his shoes somewhere and was padding about on the carpet in black socks.

"Thank you, Mr President," Ryan said, his tone soothing. "For the job offer, and the invitation."

"If you take the job, there'll be plenty more invitations." Kearney helped himself to a beer – apparently not his first, Ryan noted – and slumped back down on the couch. The shabby room was downbeat and friendly after the formal splendor of some of the White House apartments, and Ryan could understand exactly why it would be the kind of place a man would retreat to when he was too tired to string two coherent thoughts together. "Whenever I'm not at some dinner or working my way through a stack of papers."

"Thank you, sir."

"Uh-huh. You swim?"

"Yes, sir. At least, I used to. I haven't, for a while."

"I like to go swimming. I'd want you with me."

"Yes, sir. I'd be happy to."

"Play golf?"

"No, Mr President, I never have."

"Ah." Kearney registered a momentary disappointment, then shrugged it off. "You can learn. Badminton?"

"I'm not very good."

"You'll get better. Tennis?"

"Reasonable," Ryan laughed.

"Good. My daughter likes to play, and I don't have the time to join her as often as I'd like. She has a coach, but I'd really appreciate it if you encouraged her as well."

"I'll do my best."

"You watch sports? Comedies? Science fiction? What?"

"Most kinds of sport. I'm not into NASCAR – or science fiction, I'm afraid – but I'll watch a good comedy any day."

"Are we going to get on well together, Colonel, do you think?" Kearney asked him, bluntly.

"I don't see why not, Mr President. We're both sensible men."

"Sensible?" Kearney's eyes turned fully towards him then. "You think I'm a sensible man, Colonel Ryan?"

"I hope you are, sir, if you're running my country."

"Good answer." A wave of the hand indicated the unoccupied half of the couch. "Sit down."

Ryan plunked himself down in the space beside Kearney and looked squarely into the man's lined face.

"Nervous?" Kearney asked. "Reminding yourself what I do for a living?"

"A little, Mr President," Ryan conceded, without embarrassment.

"Uh-huh. It's just a job, you know. Like being a high school principal or a sanitation engineer. Try to get past it for a moment and tell me if you think the two of us can work out how to be friends, even if it takes a little time."

"Sir," Ryan said, calmly, "now that I've met you properly, I don't think it's going to be a problem."

"No." The release of tension from Kearney's frame was unexpected and highly complimentary to his guest, as though perhaps Ryan himself was not the only one who had viewed the encounter with alarm. When he wondered what there might be about him that could unsettle a man prepared to stare down the leaders of more than half the planet's population he came up with nothing like a satisfactory answer, yet the symptoms were impossible to mistake; Kearney had been just as nervous as he was himself. "So, you want to choose a movie?"

The pile on the table was an apparently random selection of anything that might take a tired man's fancy; there were detective thrillers, comedies, sports fables, westerns from both the gritty and impossibly hygienic ends of the spectrum. Ryan's hand hovered over a cheesy rom-com, then lit with decision on something featuring car chases and girls in skimpy clothing. "Will this do?"

Kearney waved away his selection. "I don't care," he said. "Choose whatever you want to watch; I'll probably be asleep within fifteen minutes."

"Oh." And before the unwisdom of cracking a joke with the President could occur to him, he ploughed on; "Maybe something with fewer explosions, then?"

The look he received in exchange was almost unreadable, but not without an element of humor. "Chad," the President said, "the way I feel right now, you'd have to blow up the East Room just to get my attention. Trust me, I could sleep through a hurricane."

"I hope you never have to prove that, sir," replied Ryan, as he slotted the movie into the machine and settled into what seemed to have become his half of the couch.

An hour and a half later the tray of sandwiches had suffered serious depredations. Kearney, having finished his beer and got halfway through another, had survived rather longer than predicted; he had made it almost as far as the first love scene, wherein the blond secret agent – who, he remarked, dressed better than any agent of his acquaintance could afford to – had bedded the girl with more enthusiasm than might have been expected from one who knew he was fraternizing with the enemy.

Ryan watched the proceedings with a jaded eye. It was not simply that the girl did not appeal to him, or that the handsome naked backside of the leading actor's body-double was so infrequently on view; it was more the fault of the script with its empty clichés and its all-too-expected twists. The bigger the film's budget, it seemed, the smaller the proportion of the money reached the writers. An infinite number of monkeys could have done a better job. Nevertheless he gave the tissue-thin plot his full attention, challenging himself to predict what the characters would say and do and rarely being proven wrong. It was that or, as he was uncomfortably aware, let his attention wander and realize that he was alone in a room with a sleeping President, a place where in a logical world he had no business to be. Duty – if there were such a thing in a situation like this – would seem to dictate that he concentrate on the rubbish on the screen and be tactful enough not to notice the occasional snore.

It was no problem at first not to wake the man but as the evening drew on, he began to realize that he had no idea where the nearest bathroom was, and that he was effectively marooned in the middle of a house he knew nothing about and could not find his way out unaided. This was roughly the point at which Ryan started to wish that Kearney would wake up of his own accord, and mercifully in the closing minutes of the film he did so. Kearney's eyes opened and found Ryan watching him, and the grin that spread across his tired face and lighted his eyes as a result was so utterly unguarded that Ryan could hardly prevent himself grinning back. He did not understand how it was possible to be so relaxed in the company of a man who could order the life or death of millions, but when he looked into the warm pleasure in Kearney's smile he knew it was the same for him too; this could certainly be a friendship, if they had a mind to make it one.

"I guess I'd better let you get home," said Kearney, getting to his feet. "I've kept you long enough. You going to take the job?"

"Yes." No prevarication or qualification. Ryan was standing now, too, his eye-line a little lower than the President's. They both looked disreputable and untidy, and Kearney still had the remains of his by now half-sheepish grin.

"I'll have someone call you," he said. "Make arrangements to have your pets and house-plants taken care of; you may not see much of them for the next few months."

"Yes, sir."

"Thank you for this evening," Kearney added, as if thanking an escort for a date. "I haven't slept so well in a while. You've made a great start."

"Thank you, Mr President. Thank you for dinner."

Kearney chuckled. "We can do better than beer and sandwiches," he said. "Well, you'll find out. It's just nice to do something ordinary for a change, though, isn't it?"

"Yes, sir, it is." Ryan had picked up his jacket and shrugged into it, and to his astonishment found that he had lapsed so far from accepted protocol as to be adjusting his tie whilst speaking to the President. He stopped only when he realized Kearney was offering him another handshake, warmer than the first, which he took with unfeigned alacrity.

"The agents will show you out," Kearney said. "You'll soon find your way around. I'll see you Monday. Maybe we can go swimming."

"Yes, sir," Ryan smiled. "I hope so."

As Kearney opened the door and handed him into the care of a Secret Service agent, Ryan looked back over his shoulder. He was leaving behind a shambling figure with rumpled hair and no shoes, who shuffled about the untidy sitting room nibbling at a dried-up sandwich snatched from the littered table, and his heart was filled with extraordinary fondness for the man.

Well, he wouldn't be the only one. A lot of people were fond of Kearney. His job required him to inspire people to vote for him and they must at the very least be able to tolerate him; it would hardly be surprising if a few of them went further and found that they had fallen more than a little in love with him. At least, that was what might have happened if they had known the privilege of watching him wake up and been on the receiving end of that magnificent but modest smile – or if, as the Fates decreed, they were unattached gay men in the President's own age bracket.

He stopped and shook his head, feeling a wash of cold acid flooding through him. He had been so careful, so confident that this sort of thing would never happen to him again. He had thought himself armored against any more disastrous one-sided love affairs. Surely it should simply be a question of acknowledging that this man's company was delightful but that he was completely out of reach of the most enthusiastic imagination? If ever a man came fenced around with signs that read "Look, but don't touch", it was Douglas Ford Kearney.

Not, he was forced to acknowledge, that such a warning was ever likely to have an influence on the ambitious megalomaniac that was his heart. It had let him down before, and it looked as if it was planning to do so yet again.

"Everything okay, Colonel?" The agent who had been escorting him down the corridor noticed the hesitation and paused alongside him. "Did you forget something?" Her tone was solicitous.

"No," Ryan said, determinedly not glancing back again towards the now closed door. "Is he always like that?"

The agent's mouth twitched. "I should really say 'like what?', shouldn't I?" she asked. "But ... no, not usually. Maybe he just feels comfortable around you."

"I ... " Ryan began, then realized what he had been about to say. "I think I feel comfortable around him too," he confessed. "Does that sound crazy?"

"Not as crazy as you might imagine," she told him. "In fact it's probably a good thing, if you guys're going to be living in each other's pockets. I guess I'll see you on Monday, then, Colonel; Agent Cooledge will take you the rest of the way."

"Thank you, Agent ... ?"

"Hernandez."

"Thank you, Agent Hernandez." If he was going to work here, he was going to have to start learning these people's names and functions, fast. At the moment, that seemed like a formidable obstacle to be overcome; it was one of the reasons why he'd always preferred his behind-the-scenes existence – technology was a hell of a lot easier to deal with than people.

"You're welcome, Colonel, and good luck on your first day. This place can really seem like a madhouse until you get used to it, but when you do … "

"It's better?" he speculated, not entirely hopefully.

"Oh, no, sir," she smiled back. "It's only when you really get used to it that you realize it's actually completely insane."

2.

By the time Ryan returned to his apartment it was too late to do anything but strip off his uniform and fall wearily into bed. Unfortunately, however, it failed to have the desired effect. Rather than the expected descent into exhausted slumber, he found himself chasing odd ideas and peculiar illusions through a bewildered half-sleep, his mind wandering carpeted corridors lined with anonymous doors, in and out of offices staffed by faceless suits. It was as if the mechanisms in his brain had failed to process his visit to the White House effectively and were even now struggling to assimilate its implications.

At two in the morning, he dragged himself out of bed, showered under the hottest water he could stand and sat in front of his TV watching an inane talk-show punctuated by commercials for things he couldn't imagine anyone wanting. He wondered whether the President was getting any sleep, having recognized symptoms of borderline insomnia in the man. While there was undoubtedly reassurance in knowing that the individual responsible for the safety of the world was awake and capable of making decisions if need be, on the whole he felt he would prefer to have a President able to switch off entirely, who could sleep soundly and awake refreshed. That was, of course, exactly what he would have liked to be able to do himself.

Six hours of dreamless oblivion later he opened his eyes to discover a green cartoon thing on the screen talking to a pink cartoon thing in high-pitched Spanish. His telephone was ringing. With wooden fingers he fumbled it to his ear, muted the toon-a-thon, and received instructions for the first day of his new employment without his higher brain taking any appreciable part in the proceedings whatever.

The next morning he presented himself in civilian clothing to Agent Cooledge at the outer perimeter and was given a security briefing. When he emerged he was conducted to one of the staff Mess facilities and wrapped himself around a sandwich and a cup of coffee. Cooledge, a thin-faced African American, was not big on conversation but passed the time with polite small talk until, with relief, the pair spied Agent Hernandez making her way towards them.

"Olivia." Cooledge greeted her with a reserved kind of smile.

"Thank you, Joel. Colonel Ryan, you're going to have the pleasure of my company for a couple hours now; Agent Cooledge has to get back to the President."

"You say that as if he was more important," Ryan told her, trusting he had remembered her sense of humor correctly.

"We let him pretend he is." Then, as Cooledge made himself scarce, she settled down beside Ryan. "How're you holding up?" she asked.

"I honestly have no idea. I'm not stupid, I know I'll be able to cope with all this stuff eventually, but right now … it's like walking through a maze of mirrors."

"Yeah, we all feel like that the first day. You should have seen the President. If he didn't have Joel and me keeping him on the straight and narrow he'd have got himself lost inside the first hour."

"You're on his personal protection team?"

"Joel is. I'm usually with the First Lady, but we kind of rotate duties so nobody gets stale. It just happens to be my turn to stay here this week while the rest of the family goes to Florida."

"To Mrs Kearney's parents?" His day off had not been totally wasted; Google, as always, had been his friend.

"Right. You'll like them. Her father's a riot. Seventy-five going on thirteen. Berry adores him."

"I'm supposed to play tennis with her," he told her. "I've never had much to do with kids."

"You'll be fine. Treat her like a sawed-off adult; don't patronize or talk down; listen, once in a while. Berry takes after her grandfather. She likes to be the center of attention."

Weakly Ryan shook his head, wondering what the hell he was getting into. "She sounds exhausting."

"She is. They all are. You'll get used to it. Eventually."

"Or die in the attempt?" he grimaced.

"Possibly," was the comforting response. "Believe me, Colonel, there are plenty of worse ways to go."

The afternoon continued the way the morning had begun; he met people and talked about his health, his family, his ambitions in the service; he was passed back and forth between Cooledge and Hernandez and an anemic-looking agent named Bennett, route-marched along carpets and through lobbies and asked to sit and wait on every level of the building, all the time wondering what in Heaven's name he was supposed to be doing. A little after four, when he had given up hope of getting an answer and was idly observing the changing pattern of clouds through a window, he was startled from his reverie by the sudden irruption into the room of a party of half a dozen men, at the head of which was the President.

"Chad, I'm sorry to have kept you waiting."

He was on his feet in a second, all confusion. "That's all right, sir, I … "

An abrupt wave of the hand from the President silenced him. "I'm running late. I only have forty-five minutes before the Russian Ambassador. Want to take a swim?"

"I don't – Yes, sir, I'd like to."

"Good. Come with me. We keep shorts and things down there for guests," Kearney added, "if that's what you're worried about."

"Yes, sir, it was."

"Okay, let's go."

With the swift precision of a motorcade, the little group marched out of the room, Ryan at the President's side, and was convoyed to an elevator and down into the bowels of the building.

"I only get one chance at this every day," the President remarked, as though he was not the man who called the shots. "They keep the pool clear between four and five. The rest of the time it belongs to my family and the senior staff, although I guess if I came down at midnight they might let me in. I should try that some time."

The elevator opened into an antechamber leading to a communal changing room with cubicles opening off it. The floor was tiled but the walls and benches were cedar-clad, giving the whole the atmosphere of a luxurious health club.

"You can get a sauna here," Kearney remarked. "Whatever." The echelon of agents moved past them and scanned the room, eyes never still, then returned to the doorway.

"All clear, sir," one of them said.

Kearney nodded. "Don't call me unless the sky falls in," he said, and yanked savagely at his tie to remove it. "I change out here," he added, in Ryan's direction. "Those little cabins are too small, I keep hitting my elbows on the wall. Help yourself to something to wear, there's a whole selection."

For the first time, Ryan noticed that two places had been set in the changing room, at opposite sides of a fretwork screen that ran through the middle. Kearney obviously had his preferred space, whereas towels and shampoo and half a dozen sets of swim-wear in the appropriate size had been left out for Ryan. The snap of the President's belt-buckle shook him from his paralyzed condition and spurred him into action; if this man had no qualms about changing his clothing alongside someone he had just met, it hardly seemed appropriate for Ryan to manifest them.

A pair of denim-look shorts seemed the least worst option available and by the time he had got into them, he was bizarrely aware that the President was waiting in the doorway wearing a similar garment in black.

"C'mon," he said, "I don't have all day. I'm supposed to be making nice with a former KGB Kommisar. The man has the worst teeth I've ever seen, and his breath stinks like a dead hedgehog."

Ryan dropped whatever it was he'd been fiddling with and almost ran across the dimpled floor. The pool appeared before his eyes, blue and gleaming, under lights which mimicked the sun of a summer day and surrounded by a mural of an English garden. He did not have time to notice much, however, as Kearney threw a shallow dive from the pool's edge and was a considerable distance away before he surfaced. Rather than await what he knew would be a barbed remark about his tardiness, Ryan followed him with less elegance and far more noise, letting the silky warmth of the water block his senses for a few blissful moments. Then he pushed back into the world of air to find Kearney watching him with undisguised amusement.

"Graceful," the President remarked, gray eyebrows lifting.

"I'm out of practice," said Ryan, defensively.

"Uh-huh." Kearney moved closer, casting an appraising glance over his scarred upper torso. "Taking two bullets through your shoulder wouldn't have helped," he said. "Now I can see why you were in the hospital all that time. It must hurt like crazy."

"It's not so bad. They rebuilt the joint completely, and I've had four or five skin grafts."

"Yeah, well, they're no fun." Kearney paused. "My wife was a trauma nurse when I met her. She used to specialize in burns."

"Oh."

Yet there was more to this conversation than was immediately apparent, something about the way the President bit his lip as if to make sure he didn't say anything inappropriate. His expression was troubled, his eyes lost and far away.

"You know," he said, quietly, "when you take this job – my job – you kind of have to accept that people are going to die in your name, whether you like it or not, but most of the time they're people you never met and hundreds of miles away. You never think it'll be somebody whose hand you just shook, or that you're going to have to watch them shot down in front of you. I understand you feel very strongly about what happened to Corrado and I want you to know I'm no happier about it than you are. I want to make amends, both to his family and to you."

"Thank you, sir." Ryan held the President's gaze for a moment, then let his eyes drop. "But it really isn't necessary."

"I know you didn't think about it," Kearney said. "I know you'd do it again. All my security guys say the same thing. That isn't the point."

"No, sir."

"The guy would have killed me," the President went on. "That's just how it is. We can argue about why it happened, but the bottom line is he intended to shoot me and you stopped him. You gave me back the rest of my life, and I'm inclined to take it personally. It's why I'd like you to stay around and enjoy the privileges that go with this crazy job."

Mutely, Ryan nodded.

"Okay." The now-familiar one-sided grin returned. "I'm going to be busy for the next couple of days. Get yourself settled in, talk to Mitch's assistant about golf lessons, come and watch another movie Friday evening. The First Lady will be home on Saturday and then I have to go to South America, so this is going to be the last chance for a while."

"Thank you, Mr President. I'll do that."

"We'll see if we can't do better than pastrami sandwiches this time," Kearney teased, sinking back into the water and beginning a lazy backstroke to the far end of the pool. "Maybe I'll even send out for a pizza."

The days that followed were even more confusing. While Kearney and his senior staff were taken up with receptions, speeches and briefings, Ryan was allocated a desk in a narrow room that gave every appearance of having been converted from a pantry. Painting the walls a vile shade of yellow had not improved its looks at all and the meager furniture was just as lacking in style, although at least functional.

By the end of the third day, he was being included, albeit peripherally, in some of Mitch Booth's meetings. He mostly sat around on couches alongside junior staffers quite as much at sea as he was himself, wondering whether it would be appropriate to take notes but relying instead on a memory that was going to let him down one of these days. It was like skulking at the back of the class, being the kid who really, really didn't want the teacher to notice him.

On the Tuesday of the second week, one of these congregations ended with Booth turning sharply to him, a huge grin on his face.

"Chad, I'd like you to tag along while I talk to the Vice President. It's about time you two met."

Ryan's eyebrows lifted. He didn't know much about the Vice President but he'd always had the distinct impression he was Kearney's opposite in almost every respect, and for that reason suspected it would be difficult to like him. Indeed, first impressions tended to support this view; when they were ushered into the dark paneled office in use by Kearney's deputy, it was to be greeted by a man as unlike the Chief Executive as it was possible to be. Howard Maddocks, Secretary of Commerce in a previous administration, had the crumpled, bad-tempered face of an over-indulged lapdog. Approaching his seventieth year, he was of an actuarial disposition with a mania for detail which was all the more aggravating for being indispensable. He regarded Ryan with overt suspicion.

"Mr Vice President, this is Charles Ryan."

"Ryan." Maddocks nodded with the minimum of civility.

"Sir."

"Well, sit down, both of you." The chairs were hard and unwelcoming. "What have you got, Mitch?"

Booth slid a sheaf of photographs across the desk. "A supposedly peaceful petrochemical plant in the Tien Shan mountains," he said. "It took them fifteen months to build the railway and two and a half years to start producing something, although at the moment we're not sure what. We've had various people inside at various times, but they keep on disappearing."

"Hmmm." Maddocks' small dark eyes fixed firmly on his two visitors. "Have you seen these pictures, Ryan?"

"No, sir."

Maddocks pushed them back to him. "Tell me what you think."

Ryan looked through them. "Open freight trucks go in empty and come out full?" he asked, tapping at the image of a large gray rectangle.

"Apparently," Maddocks nodded.

"With what?"

"Our experts say it looks like railway ballast. It goes to a big freight yard nine hundred miles east where they spend the next three months playing 'Three-card Monte' with it. Any idea what they're doing?"

Ryan grimaced. "I wouldn't like to say but there has to be at least a possibility that they're tunneling into the mountain. Where they're going, and why, I couldn't begin to guess." He looked up in time to catch Maddocks and Booth exchanging a glance, and to notice that Maddocks's mouth had compressed into a fine, pensive line.

"All right," the Vice President said, slowly. "No need to remind you that this is confidential."

"No, sir, I understand that."

Maddocks got to his feet and walked around the desk, signifying that the interview was over. He held out his hand for the photographs, which Ryan returned with a respectful nod.

"It won't come as any surprise, Colonel, that I disagreed with the President's decision to appoint you. Well, I made my protest – and he over-ruled me. You're here."

"Sir."

"Show me you can do your job adequately; that's all I need from you."

"Yes, sir."

"And remember this; there are a dozen Deputy NSAs to every Vice President. Get that tattooed on your hide, you won't go far wrong."

"I'll bear it in mind, Mr Vice President. Thank you for the advice."

"Presidents don't make new friends, Colonel; that's why they take care of the old ones. Mitch, ask my guys to come in when you leave, will you?"

"Sir."

The two of them turned in synchrony, and had passed into the outer office and through into the corridor before either dared to take another breath.

"And don't let the door hit you in the butt on the way out," Booth muttered, not quite inaudibly. "He's a peach, isn't he?"

"He does seem rather unsympathetic," conceded Ryan, mildly.

"Yeah. And that's one of the nicest things I've ever heard said about him. You remember what JFK said about Johnson?"

"That he'd rather have him inside the tent pissing out than outside pissing in?"

"That's the one. That's why we had Howard Maddocks on the ticket, and it's also why we're keeping him at the next election. His approval rating's higher than the President's. An attempted assassination usually brings a bump in the polls, but we lost ground because we had to shoot Corrado. Maddocks is the only thing keeping us above the waterline now. We can't afford to lose him."

"So that was what you meant about having enemies?"

Booth paused. "You have to admit – if you're going to have an enemy, you couldn't have made a better choice." His flippant mood vanished, however, as he added; "It's not you he dislikes, Chad, it's the thought of you. He's got this whole scenario down as a cheap publicity stunt."

"He was testing me," Ryan surmised.

"He was. He can't believe that if you were any good at your job you wouldn't have come to our notice sooner – and he's got a point; you stayed comprehensively off our radar and Maddocks can't work out why. He doesn't understand anybody who isn't driven by personal ambition. Being content with what you've got is a concept he can't assimilate."

Lines of bewilderment furrowed Ryan's brow. "I got where I wanted to be," he protested, "and I stayed. I didn't want anything else. I'd achieved my ambition and I was happy. What's odd about that? "

Booth shook his head sadly. "As far as the Vice President's concerned," he answered, "pretty nearly everything."

That afternoon, and on the two following, the President's schedule over-ran into the slot set aside for swimming. On the first occasion, Ryan waited within hailing distance of the Oval Office but the summons did not come. When the hour was over, he returned to his office and to the paperwork Booth had been funneling in his direction, but found it difficult to concentrate.

The next day, he again settled down to wait for the President, only to be chased away within five minutes by the man himself.

"I can't make it today," Kearney told him. "You go alone."

"Actually, sir, I probably have work to do."

"No, you should go." A casual slap to his shoulder. "I want you to. In fact, we should just agree to meet down there in future; that way you'll still get your swim even if I don't."

"Yes, sir. If you think that's a good idea."

"I do. Maybe you can find a way to do enough relaxing for both of us."

"I'll do my best, Mr President."

And so he did, but it was not the same. One agent accompanied him to the basement and waited for him outside, although they were both aware that it was a total waste of time, and changing alone in the big room was an isolating experience. When Ryan plunged into the water the echo of his splash seemed to bounce forlornly around the walls, impeded by contact with no body but his own; when, after a dozen laps and tired of his own company, he returned to the changing room, the President's clothing and toiletries had been tidied away in his absence. Without them, he felt lonelier than ever.

The day after that, he did not change but sat on the cedar bench and waited for the hour to pass. Somehow, he could not bring himself to enter the water. His continued presence seemed to deter the invisible elf from coming in to remove the President's belongings, however, and he was left in peace. At the end of the hour, he returned to his canary cage and quietly got on with his work, without ever asking himself what on Earth he had been doing or thinking about during the hiatus.

He was expecting the President's invitation to watch a movie to be rescinded as well, but later that evening the phone on his desk rang and a familiar voice asked in some irritation where he the heck was.

"In my office," he answered, stupidly, and then laughed in embarrassment. "I'm sorry, Mr President, I thought you'd be too busy."

"I'm only too busy when I say I'm too busy," was the mild rebuke. Then, as though to tempt him, "I ordered fried chicken, since my wife's not around to nag me, but if you don't get here quickly I'm going to eat the whole bucket by myself."

"Well, I really should try to save you from that," Ryan told him. "I'll be right there."

Briskly he put the phone down, tidied away the contents of his desk, and virtually sprinted through the corridors. A couple of minutes later he was opening the door to the shambles of a room on the upper floor.

"Movie night," the President said. "You nearly missed it."

"I'm sorry. I didn't realize ... "

"You were having way too much fun reading about North Korean business interests in Paraguay?"

"I was, sir, I must admit."

"Well, that's tough, Colonel, because I'm going to pull rank and make you drink beer and watch stoner comedy. Park it," he added, with a smile. "You have my official permission not to think about work at all for the next couple of hours."

By the end of the film it was closing in on midnight and the President's mood was quieter. He lounged back with his feet resting on the edge of a low table, an almost-empty beer bottle clutched in one hand, and the parade of silliness passed in front of him without comment. When the screen finally went dark he switched off and let the remote control drop slowly from his fingers, apparently reluctant for the evening to end.

"I'm told you didn't swim today. My spies say you didn't even go in the pool."

"You're spying on me?" The incredulous response had forced its way out before Ryan could recollect exactly who it was he was talking to. Then, in some chagrin, he went on; "I mean, of course you are, I don't know why I said that."

"Hey, I wanted to be sure you're settling in okay." The President paused, awkwardly. "Anyway, since neither of us got our swim at the regular time, how about we just go down there now?"

"Really?"

"Why not?" Jumping to his feet, Kearney opened the door. "Agent Bennett?"

"Yes, Mr President?"

"There won't be anybody in the pool this time of night, will there?"

"No, sir. The facility will be closed up."

"But you have the code for the door, right?"

"Yes, sir."

"Good. Then we're going swimming. Notify whoever it is you have to notify, will you?"

"I'll advise my superior, sir. Are you ready to leave?"

"Just about. Come along, Chad; you won't need your jacket."

The building was nothing like deserted as they passed through it, with communications staff and cleaners making the place almost as populous as it was during the day, but the lighting was subdued and so were the voices. Those who, either by choice or necessity, worked through the hours of darkness seemed on the whole less extrovert and more composed than their daytime counterparts and not so given to extremes of emotion.

Theirs was a peaceful existence, enviable in that it appeared to progress without interruption. More reassuringly still, nobody took the slightest notice of the two of them as they and their Secret Service detail passed unobtrusively by.

It was Bennett who admitted them to the changing room and Bennett who found the lights. After a moment's confusion he switched on just enough for them to find their way around, and set the ventilation humming in the background. A bale of clean towels sat on the end of one bench ready for the morning, but a quick glance showed no trunks or shorts in any of the obvious places.

"You object to skinny-dipping?" Kearney asked, abruptly.

Unable to speak, Ryan shook his head. He grabbed a towel from the bale and took up his place in the room, and the President did the same.

"Michael? Lock that door and stay outside."

"Yes, sir."

For the next few moments it was all a flurry of untidiness and clothing discarded any old how, and then the sound of large bare feet across a tiled floor. Ryan was about to wrap the towel around his waist when he glanced up, saw a surprisingly tanned backside disappearing in the direction of the pool and heard an almighty splash; the President's towel still lay where he had left it on the bench.

Ryan left his own behind and followed, feeling as if his feet and hands had suddenly grown to monumental proportions and his genitals shriveled away to nothing. Public nudity was one aspect of service life he'd always struggled with; he could do it, of course, but the more senior he became the less the necessity and the more grateful he was. He felt ungainly and wrong around other men's nakedness, as if they were somehow all better constructed and more worthy to be looked at than himself. Not that he wanted to look, especially, since being caught looking at another man's body had the potential to lead to disaster – and in present company it would be safer not to let his eyes stray at all. He hoped that would count as courtesy or discretion on his part, but he could not quite distance himself from a voice in his head that repeatedly and unequivocally called it cowardice.

Under low lighting, the pool room gave the impression of some mysterious subterranean grotto. The interplay of light and water threw strange rippling shadows on the ceiling, and a thin haze of mist sat on a surface as green and corrugated as antique glass. Ryan slid into the water as gently it as if it had been sleep, letting it fold itself around him with the sensuousness of silk sheets, luxuriating in its slow caress across his skin.

When he rose to the surface and pushed wet hair out of his eyes, he draped himself over the grab-rail at the side of the pool and tilted his head to haul in a long, deep, relaxing breath.

A quiet voice came steadily to him out of the gloom.

"I should have tried this years ago," said Kearney. He was several yards away, his body half-turned, his eyes concealed, yet he seemed so comfortable in the water that he might have been Poseidon himself. "You're a bad influence."

What on Earth was he to say to that, with formality so out of place and intimacy so unthinkable? "I'm sorry," was the best he could manage, and it sounded utterly inadequate.

"Don't be. I knew you'd be good for me, I just didn't know how. I told Kirsten; sometimes all the planning and analyzing in the world doesn't matter a row of beans and you have to go with gut instinct." Kearney stopped speaking, lowering himself so that only his head and shoulders were visible above the waterline.

"Yes, Mr President."

Unconscious of doing so, Ryan mirrored the move. Now they were two disembodied torsos, staring at one another across an infinite distance like classical marble busts in a sculpture gallery.

Something about the forbidden nature of the encounter was taking root in his mind, something he could not diffuse with humor. Had this been a different workplace, he might have shrugged it off; he might have neutralized the seductive power of the moment with some piece of clowning or incompetence and always be known to history as a harmless idiot. But this was the White House and what happened here tended not to be powered by random chance. There was something about this situation, therefore, that Kearney had either engineered or at least acquiesced in. That being the case, Ryan was inclined to flow with it, to accept it for what it was – a once in a lifetime experience so completely out of the ordinary that when he woke up in the morning he would not believe it had happened. And maybe, given the dreamlike ambiance, that was exactly how it was supposed to be.

"You know, Chad, when we're naked, I think it would be okay for you to call me 'Doug'."

"It would?" But the implications of 'when we're naked' were disturbing. His body gave a hopeful pulse, a sudden thrill surging through his nerve-endings to settle in his balls and stir desires that made him grateful for the distance between them. He did not want to be seen by his boss in this embarrassingly aroused condition. "Does that mean we're going to be doing this again?"

"I hope so," returned Kearney. "Every chance we get."

The notion filled Ryan with delight and horror both. It felt good to be together, as if there were a real connection between them, but who was he to be here, alone and naked, with the most powerful man in the world? Whoever got to see a President without his clothes – his physician, his wife, his lover – it would not normally be some unknown Air Force officer. Kearney must be very sure of his loyalty, must be convinced no word of this would ever leak out. Kearney must trust him beyond anything their brief acquaintance could possibly seem to have justified.

Ryan knew his practical value to the administration was virtually nil; the interview with Maddocks had made that clear. He was useful, and that was fine, but he was no high-flying intellectual. In company with these men, he was merely a bumbling Watson whose function was to have things explained to him. As far as undemanding companionship went, Kearney would have done just as well with a Labrador retriever.

Yet there was more. There was an undercurrent of muted sexuality, an exotic and dangerous intimacy. Had they been any other two men he would have known what that meant; he would have known that, married or not, his companion was expressing an interest, and he would have been happy to respond. Kearney, rangy and fit for his age, closely matched his template for a lover; it would give him enormous pleasure

30

to revel in the physicality of the man, to run his hands along the lean limbs and over the flat stomach, to feed on the fascinating mouth. He could have fallen into this man's arms rejoicing, if only his name had not been Douglas Ford Kearney.

But he would not allow himself to think about it. Kearney might not be above flirting with an employee, but there were reasons why no such infatuation should ever be allowed to take root. Kearney had a wife, a child, responsibilities and duties that outweighed the temptations of momentary dalliance.

It was a relief to put such thoughts away completely, to acknowledge that nothing more than transient lust had troubled his evening. It was clear that he did not really desire Kearney; he could not possibly desire him, because of who and what he was. No matter how lonely he might be, no matter how closely he might work with him, he could never allow himself to feel about any President of the United States the way he had been afraid he was beginning to feel about this one.

Not, at least, if he were to have any hope at all of staying sane.

3.

Any fallout Ryan might have been expecting from that evening completely failed to materialize, and the return of the First Lady and her daughter over the weekend meant that the President was not in evidence again until Monday when he was preoccupied with preparing for the trip to South America. Swimming was cut to a half-hour, during which conversation was minimal. Gone was the comfortable familiarity that had prevailed at their previous meeting, and instead Kearney seemed to have retreated behind a shell of diffidence that made him appear awkward and formal and older than his years. It was only when they were preparing to leave that he managed to introduce any topic at all, and then he said, as though it was so unimportant that he had almost forgotten, "By the way, my wife wants to meet you."

"I'd be honored." But the prospect filled him with alarm.

"Tomorrow. She's doing a charity thing – one of her causes, I forget which. Show up on time, smile, ask intelligent questions, don't let me down, okay?"

"Yes, sir."

"I probably won't see you until I get back. We won't have a chance to swim tomorrow and I'm leaving early Wednesday." He sounded as if he regretted it.

"I hope you have a pleasant journey, Mr President."

Kearney groaned. "Chad, you don't know what you're saying. You know what happens when you get three South American Presidents together?"

"No, sir. What happens?"

Relaxing a little, the President slapped his shoulder and steered him into the elevator cabin. "You get six opinions and two revolutions. I'm not sure any of those guys will be in a job this time next year but I'm not sure I will either. Some things are an almighty waste of time and you need to acknowledge that going in."

"Yes, Mr President."

"While I'm away, I want you to liaise with the Vice President's office about Kyrgyzstan. Mitch tells me you said all the right things when he talked to you, so I've asked him to keep you in the loop from now on. Let's make sure we get full use out of your talents for however long we're lucky enough to have you, shall we?" The elevator stopped moving, the doors slid open and the President stepped out. "If it looks like I'll be back at a reasonable hour, I'll call you."

"Thank you, sir."

Ryan watched him march away along a narrow line of carpet bordered by gleaming inlaid floors, then returned to his office and made some attempt to study charitable causes close to the First Lady's heart. It was not long, however, before his peace and quiet was interrupted by the appearance of a very self-possessed young lady in bead-spattered pink jeans and a lurid pink tee-shirt.

"You're Chad," she said. "My dad's friend."

He glanced up. Habit had already taught him that there should be an agent in the immediate vicinity, and sure enough Hernandez was just outside the door wearing a highly amused look on her face.

"I am." He had got to his feet automatically. "Miss Kearney."

"Berry. You're going to play tennis with me. I go to Senator Tack's house in Arlington; it's quiet there and the agents like it."

He looked at her properly. There was not an ounce of spare fat on her anywhere and she looked as if she wouldn't cast a shadow. He, on the other hand, was carrying an extra few pounds after a mostly sedentary convalescence and had never – except for that one occasion – been especially quick on his feet. He was also far enough past forty not to be an ideal tennis partner for an energetic child.

"I'll do my best, but I can't help thinking it won't be much of a contest."

She grimaced at him. "You're assuming I'm any good."

He smiled back. "Well, I know I'm not."

"Neither's my dad. Maybe you should play with him instead." It was a stretch, but he managed to dismiss the idea that there was any deliberate double-entendre in her words.

"Maybe."

She was wandering around the room, trailing her fingers along the edge of his desk, picking up briefing books but knowing better than to examine anything except a snow-globe paperweight containing plastic tropical fish and plastic coral. "I don't like this room," she said. "They painted it that color to brighten it up. It's like custard. Doesn't it make you feel sick?"

"A bit," he acknowledged.

"You could ask them to change it."

The idea had not occurred to him. "What color would you suggest?"

"Oh God, anything," she said. "White. Gray. Pink."

"Not pink."

"Why not?"

"It's not a manly color. I'm not sure your father would approve."

"Huh. That's his problem. I like pink."

"So I see. And I do, too, but perhaps not on my office walls."

"Well, okay, then, have white. Or gray Or green." She stopped then, running out of ideas quickly. He watched her for a while as she checked out the lack of a view from his window and then, since she didn't seem inclined to speak again, he felt obliged to continue the conversation.

"Did you and your mother have a good flight back from Florida?"

Berry yawned. "It was okay. We were mostly talking about my birthday."

"Oh, yes, that's soon, isn't it? Will you be having a party?"

"Yes. Mom said I should ask you."

"I'm sorry?"

"Ask you. To the party." From a pocket in her jeans she brought out a small invitation card upon which his name had been carefully written in juvenile script. *Berry Kearney requests the pleasure of your company.*

"Oh." Nonplussed, he was at a loss for a response. When he could think again, he glanced in Olivia's direction and saw that she was nodding reassurance. "I'm sorry, I mean, I'd love to be there – if the First Lady doesn't mind."

"You know she hates to be called that, right?" asked Berry. "She says it's patriarchal and chauvinistic." She spoke so confidently that he had no doubt she understood the meaning of the words, and began to be afraid of the intensity she would be capable of with another five years of political education under her belt.

"Really? No, I didn't know. Perhaps I should say ... if *your mother* doesn't mind? After all, I haven't met her yet. In fact, that's happening tomorrow."

"I know." Berry shook her head, her father's determination clearly written in the line of her jaw. "But Mom likes you anyway because Dad says you're easy to have around. He says he wished he'd known you ten years ago, and then he wouldn't be in this stupid mess."

"What stupid mess?"

"This stupid White House mess, I guess. I don't know. He says he's thinking of asking people not to vote for him again in November, just so he can get some peace. Sometimes he says," she concluded, not looking in his direction at all, "that he wishes you hadn't pushed him out of the way that time."

"Oh."

"I know he's joking really, but he shouldn't say it anyway."

He would not allow himself to think too much about the implications of that – not yet, at least, while she was still in the room – but the bleakness of the sentiment shocked him. Perhaps he was beginning to understand what value he might have to Kearney and his family; perhaps all he needed to do was blunt the edge of the President's despair.

"His job must get frustrating at times," he temporized.

"Yeah, it does," responded the President's daughter. "See, I knew you'd understand. So, will you come to the party?"

"Yes," he said, trying to summon up an expression of delight and gratitude appropriate to the honor. "I'm looking forward to it."

Later that evening, he became aware of Olivia Hernandez once more looming outside his door.

"Don't worry," she said, "Berry's with her mother in the Residence. Joel's looking after them. I just came back to find out if you were okay. Looks like you don't get invited to a lot of kids' parties; no nephews and nieces, huh?"

"Not one. Is this the kind of thing where I need to bring a gift?"

"Oh, you bet it is. But talk to Angela, Mrs Kearney's secretary; she probably has something stashed in a drawer somewhere for emergencies."

"I have to see her tomorrow anyway," he responded with a shrug. "So that she can introduce me to the First Lady. Her office sent over a lot of interesting stuff about Mrs Kearney's agenda."

"Yeah." Olivia parked herself on the corner of his desk and glanced over the paperwork he had been perusing. "*Mèdecins Sans Frontières*, that's her favorite cause. You know she used to work in a burn unit and he was a fire-fighter, right? That's how they met. He worked his way up through union politics and she pushed him every step of the way. She still likes to be hands-on, though, which is why she keeps up her professional accreditation. She does volunteer work whenever she can, usually in some war zone or other. The woman's indomitable, Chad; she'd make a great President herself. In fact, he's seriously tried to talk her into it more than once."

He was looking at her with apprehension in his eyes. "Is there a single member of this family who isn't terrifying?" he asked, concerned.

"Hmmm," replied the agent, with a reassuring smile, "let me see. The President, the First Lady, Berry … they're all pretty formidable. I don't think the cat's any great intellect, but then with cats you never know. Could turn out he's been the power behind the throne the whole time. Yeah, I think you're really going to have to watch your step around him, Chad."

By morning, Ryan had finished familiarizing himself with Kirsten Kearney's agenda and showed up at the MSF reception in the Rose Room in plenty of time to listen to the speeches. Afterwards, when a suitable interval presented itself and the First Lady's secretary performed the necessary introduction, she presented him with a formal flourish that left him feeling at a massive disadvantage.

Kearney's wife was fifteen years younger than her husband, slim and tidy without being outrageously fashionable. Her hair was an intermediate shade between blonde and red, which in some cultures would have been called 'ginger' and seemed to speak for a Celtic heritage.

She was businesslike and charming to her guests, but when she turned to him her manner became less guarded and she did not trouble to conceal that she found him intriguing.

"A pleasure to meet you, Colonel. I've heard so much about you."

"Thank you, ma'am. Nothing bad, I hope?"

"Almost all of it. How are you getting on with my husband?"

"Very well, ma'am, thank you."

"You feel like you've known him for years?"

The remark took him by surprise, but there was no denying the accuracy of the observation. "As a matter of fact, I do."

"I know. Doug has that effect on people. He's an easy guy to be around, once you get past what he does for a living. I gather you met my daughter yesterday?"

"Yes. She kindly invited me to her party."

"I'm not sure it was a kindness," was the cynical response. "There'll be eighty teenagers and the clothes and music will make you feel a hundred years old. But I assure you my husband will be very glad to see you there; he likes to show up and be the dutiful father but there's never anybody for him to talk to. It'll be two hours of your life that you'll never get back but Doug will appreciate it, and so will Berry. Some of her friends actually think you're really cute."

"They don't!" He was appalled.

"You're a non-threatening older man, Colonel," laughed the First Lady, "which makes you a status symbol with her crowd. Don't get too used to it, it'll soon be over." She stopped, then smiled winningly at him. "Actually I have a favor of my own to ask. I'm going to be volunteering at a burn unit part of next month and my husband's schedule is insane while I'm away. Do you think you could visit Berry in Florida at some point, maybe take her out for lunch or to a movie? She adores my parents and they adore her, but after a week or two they grate on each other's nerves. She'll have her agents with her; all you need to do is co-ordinate your plans with them."

"Of course." Since he was already in the habit of considering every request from the Kearney family almost as an order, it did not occur to him that he could have reason to decline; nevertheless the prospect was alarming. Olivia's words, however, had stood him in good stead; treating Berry as if she were an adult of slightly reduced stature seemed to be working so far. "How difficult can it be?"

"I can see you don't have children," Kirsten Kearney smiled. "Believe me, it has its drawbacks. But it's probably not as exhausting as looking after Doug. I'd like you to do that while I'm away, too; help him relax if you can. You've made a great start, there's a real difference in his mood. He was ready to bite the heads off bulldogs before you arrived, but he's beginning to mellow out now. You must have realized how much he hates his job?"

"Oh." This seemed the kind of confidence he should really not have been party to, but there was no precedent in his experience for warning a First Lady not to divulge her family's secrets. "I didn't know he felt so strongly."

"Passionately. He wouldn't run again if there was any other alternative, but there isn't. I guarantee you he's going to loathe every single minute of that second term."

"I'd hate to think ... " Ryan began, then stopped again. "Maybe it won't be as bad as he's expecting?"

"Maybe." She did not sound as if she believed it. "But anyway, he's got plans for when he leaves office, most of them to do with never setting foot in this place again." She took his arm, drew him aside from the gathering, lowered her tone. "Has he told you about the house his aunt left him?"

"No." He didn't know whether to be more surprised that Kearney hadn't mentioned it, or that his wife had.

"It's his favorite toy. It's up in Vermont, on a big old piece of land, and one day Doug's planning to go up there with a truckload of lumber and a set of power tools and put it back together all by himself. Anything he doesn't already know how to do, he'll learn from a book as he goes along."

"That sounds ... a challenge."

"Yes, and it might take him the rest of his life – but he'd rather be working with his hands than sitting around talking to people who don't listen. Get him to tell you about it some time and you'll see he's got his work cut out; the roof leaks, there are rats in summer, and it's under six feet of snow in winter."

"If I may say so, ma'am, you don't sound very enthusiastic."

The First Lady shook her head. "Chad," she said, "it's my husband's project, not mine. It's a mile and a half from the road, has no proper plumbing, the windows don't fit and the furniture went out of style in the Hoover administration. We spent what felt like a month there one night when Berry was about seven, and that was enough for me." She paused, watching his face in amusement. "I don't go near the place if I can possibly avoid it."

"Oh." He could scarcely keep the disappointment out of his tone. "I was thinking it sounded a great place for a family," he explained.

"Maybe it will be when it's finished, but at the moment my daughter likes her comforts. She's not used to roughing it any more than I am. But you'd better be careful about expressing an interest, Colonel, or you may find yourself recruited to help. Doug needs all the slave labor he can get."

"I don't think I'd be much use," he admitted, with a smile.

"Oh, I think you might," rejoined the First Lady, the look on her face suggesting that she had heard exactly what she wanted to hear. "Doug gets lonely and works too hard, and he needs someone to remind him to have fun. You'd be just the person for that. In fact," she added, "if we get elected to a second term, you or someone like you will be essential to make sure he gets out the other end of it alive. So you'd be doing me and the rest of the world a favor if you'd kindly plan on staying around a while."

Once the First Family had taken their departure on Wednesday – crawling, half-awake, into limousines for a pre-dawn motorcade to Andrews – life at the White House reverted to weekend mode and overburdened staff used the break to clear tasks that had been put off a little too long. In Ryan's case, this meant golf lessons with a sympathetic pro at an up-scale country club, from which he returned at the end of the first day exhausted and with aches in places that he previously had not known existed. Almost the first person he ran into in the corridor was Booth, whose manner was more relaxed than usual and who seemed to be reveling in the temporary absence of his boss.

"How was it?" he asked, breezily.

"Fine, but I'm going to be in agony tomorrow."

"No pain, no gain," Booth reminded him, around an evil grin. "Come in and talk a while." So saying, he escorted Ryan back into the airy office where he had received his introduction to the White House, and they made themselves comfortable. "Serious stuff, I'm afraid. The President's keen to involve you in this Kyrgyz business – at least, that's what we're calling it. It's so close to the Chinese border, though ... " He spread a map on his desk and tapped it with a broad finger. "There's a nuclear plant about here," he said. "Thirty miles inside China, CIA codename 'Holofernes'. You have to wonder if that's entirely coincidental."

Ryan leaned down low over the map. "Away from centers of population," he mused. "I take it we're not talking about domestic energy production?"

"Oh, they're producing energy but I doubt very much whether that's their primary purpose. It probably costs them more in transportation than it's worth, although they've made a big deal out of bringing electricity into the borderlands. Spectrographic analysis of satellite data indicates we're probably looking at large-scale production of Plutonium isotope 239 – weapons-grade, of course."

"Of course. Why is it never good news?"

"If it were, they wouldn't have to keep it secret. The quantities ... " Booth shrugged.

"I imagine we're talking about overkill?"

"On a massive scale."

"Massive scale is right." Ryan was measuring distances on the map with his thumbnail. "You realize that for this tunnel to go anywhere near Holofernes it would have to be at least eighty miles long? That's more than twice the length of the Channel Tunnel. The sheer logistics of getting a train through it would be almost as complicated as putting a guy into space."

"I know. Plus you're talking cross-border co-operation between

China and Kyrgyzstan and you know damn well the Chinese aren't doing it out of the goodness of their hearts. When they were talking about building a railway through the Torugart Pass they ended up deciding the cost was prohibitive, but that would have been a drop in the ocean compared to this. So who paid, and why? There's no way the Kyrgyz could afford it, their economy isn't on that kind of scale. Even if they were still part of the Soviet Union, I'm not sure they could ever have found the money."

"So there has to be something they have that China wants enough to go to all this trouble. What do we know of that's more valuable than Pu-239?"

"Beats me," growled Booth. "Petroleum needs a pipeline, not a railway, and they're in the wrong place geologically. Water – same argument, and anyway the Chinese wouldn't go to that amount of trouble for water when it's cheaper just to depopulate the area. Plus they've got enough in the Yarkand to keep Holofernes supplied, so I think we can take it they're not buying in water from the Kyrgyz."

"Could we be looking at Kyrgyz internal politics, then?" suggested Ryan. "They're pretty stable, aren't they, except for increasing Islamisation and discontent among ethnic minorities? Although I doubt whether they're planning to use nuclear weapons against thirty thousand unarmed Tajiks, it would be a bit too much like the sledgehammer and the nut."

"Which, of course is the problem," came the dispirited response. "There's no obvious reason, and if there was I'm not sure I'd trust it. Our people in the area are hoping to be able to analyze material brought out of the mountain, but in the meantime you should pick yourself up a copy of *Nuclear Genocide for Dummies* – I'd like you to read into Kyrgyz politics and see if you can find something everybody else has missed. See if anybody's playing factions, cultivating a relationship with China to buy himself support at home, that kind of thing. You should have time for that with the President out of town. How'd you get on with the First Lady, by the way?"

Ryan smiled. "She was very gracious," he said, automatically.

"Uh-huh. You know, Chad, I'm not a reporter. We have kind of a crazy habit around here – sometimes we like to tell one another the truth rather than offering up sound-bites."

The rebuke stung. Ryan had been perfectly sincere, but had quickly acquired the habit of a tactful blandness. "I'm sorry," he said, "but she was gracious. I didn't understand everything she said, though; in fact, it was a very odd conversation. Something to do with a house the President's renovating."

"Yeah, I've seen the place." Booth's expression indicated that he had been no more impressed than the First Lady. "It might make decent firewood, if it wasn't too wet to burn. You won't hear a good word from Kirsten about it; she was raised in Florida and it's too damned cold for her there but you're from Oregon, you won't even notice." Ryan did not respond to this, however, and after a moment Booth began again, this time in an altered tone. "You know," he said, leaning closer, "I think it may be time you and I talked about the President in a little more detail. There's something I should probably tell you, only I don't suppose it'll come as too much of a shock."

"No." Ryan had a horrible feeling he could guess what Booth was going to say, and tried to put a lid on the revelation. Friday evening should have given him a clue, of course, but he had still been too much in awe of the President to begin to believe his senses. Or perhaps he just had not wanted to admit to himself that there was anything even remotely homoerotic about the skinny-dipping scenario, because if he did he would have to decide exactly how he felt about his own place in it. These were questions he did not particularly want to face.

"Are you saying you won't be shocked, or that I shouldn't tell you?"

"Both. Neither. I don't want to have the conversation at all."

Booth leaned back in his chair, relaxing massively. "Which suggests you already know," he smiled. "He told you, huh? That's great. I hadn't realized things had progressed that far."

Ryan was shaking his head. "Nobody's told me anything. I ... may have worked things out for myself, that's all."

"Oh. That's what you guys call gaydar, is it?" The word sounded outlandish coming from the older man, as though it was a concept he had never quite been able to credit. "I didn't know that stuff really worked."

"It works." Ryan looked away. "It isn't a hundred percent reliable. Sometimes men who think they're straight give off signals too – and maybe they are and maybe they're not. Maybe they just don't know themselves as well as they think they do."

"Not a problem with Doug," Booth told him, quietly.

"No?"

"No. He knows himself perfectly well. And you should be aware that he's had more than one adventure of the not-exclusively-heterosexual variety."

"Really? I've never heard a word about that."

"No, you won't. Some of our enemies have closets of their own; it's what we politicians call mutually assured destruction. Since he met Kirsten he's been completely faithful, but there's no reason to suppose that wouldn't be subject to change if the right guy fell into his life."

Ryan looked up. "How long ago are we talking about here? High school?"

"Not so much," was the conciliatory response. "During the first marriage. You realize he was married before?"

"Yes. She's in … ?"

"New Zealand. She married a psychiatrist. It wasn't all roses between her and Doug, and this is the reason; his sexuality was kind of fluid back then. He finally made a choice when he married Kirsten, but believe me she knew exactly what she was taking on. She was aware that the day might come when she'd have to be prepared to share him."

Ryan shook his head slowly, mystified. "Why? Why would any woman agree to that?"

"I don't know, you need to ask her. Maybe half of a good man is better than all of a bad one? Or," he added, "better still, ask yourself. Would you go into a relationship with a man, knowing part of the time you'd have to share him with his wife?"

The answer was not slow in coming. "That would depend on the man."

"I'm sure it would. And we both know Doug Kearney's not an ordinary man, don't we?" Booth was watching the play and counter-play of emotions across Chad's face, openly assessing his reaction to the topic. For someone who guarded his emotional privacy as closely as Ryan, it was unnerving and not unlike the way he imagined the experience of a specimen on a microscope slide. "You'd better believe I wouldn't be telling you this without his express permission," Booth continued, quietly. "He's decided it's time you understood what you're getting into. I guess he thinks the two of you are starting to ... get along."

"We are." But it was obvious now that none of it had been accidental. The pool, the darkness, the absence of swim-wear, Kearney had arranged it all. He had wanted them to be alone, naked and intimate, and he had made it happen. And he had indicated more than once that something had been missing from his life before Ryan became part of it, which in turn suggested there was something he wanted from him. Could it really be as simple as it seemed? "Mitch, you assured me you weren't recruiting me specifically because I was gay."

"I didn't. I have to admit, though, it was a bonus."

"You offered me the job hoping that I'd have sex with the President?"

"Tell me you don't want to."

"That's irrelevant! I'm a career USAF officer, not a ten dollar hooker!"

"Yeah, and I notice you haven't walked out on me, so I'm going to assume a certain level of interest on your part. Let me lay it on the line for you, Chad. You were appointed because you're good enough, make no mistake about that; gay, straight, in an intense but monogamous relationship with the Denver Broncos – nobody cares, as long as you do your job. We don't compromise that kind of thing around here."

Ryan was looking at him, teetering on the edge of disbelief.

"Now," Booth went on, "the President likes you, and I know he'd be very happy if you were willing to let things develop between you. If that counts as pandering or procuring then I plead guilty – but you have to understand that he wouldn't have gone into this without Kirsten's knowledge. Those two don't make a move without consulting one another; they're a team."

The words were spoken in such a reasonable tone that Booth could have been talking about the weather or the price of pork bellies for all the emotional difference it made. In Ryan, however, they provoked a sense of insecurity. He could not forget Kirsten Kearney suggesting he might help her husband to relax in her absence. What, in fact, had she really been asking him to do?

"It can't be right. You don't want someone like me for something like this."

Booth laughed. It was not an unkind laugh, but a darned sight more knowing than Ryan had expected from him in the circumstances.

"I'll agree," he admitted, "that you don't seem the obvious choice. When you first walked in here I thought you were one of the most nervous guys I'd ever met, but as I've got to know you a little I've begun to realize that could be in your favor; the last thing Doug needs is someone who takes him for granted. And just so we're clear, Chad – you were his choice, not mine. He saw you on TV and told me he wanted to meet you. So, you want to take a wild guess exactly how much courage it took for him to do that? You think Presidents like to have their private feelings exposed to public scrutiny? You think they enjoy making great big fat ugly mistakes about people? But he didn't make any mistake about you, Chad, did he?"

Wordlessly, Ryan shook his head.

"No, I didn't think so. Now, I don't know if Doug understands where he's going with this, or if he'll ever follow through on it, but if he makes a move all you need to do is react. If it's welcome, great. If it's not welcome, tell him. Nobody's threatening you, nobody's coercing you; treat it like any other relationship. Your job is safe as long as you want it, or you can transfer back to your old unit with no reflection on your record. You hold all the aces, kid; you decide how you want to play 'em." He paused, then continued in a more moderate tone. "No-one expects you to throw yourself at the guy, Chad, but you don't find him physically repulsive or anything?"

"God, no!" The response was so quick and heartfelt as almost to set a seal on the discussion.

"Okay. Well, in that case, Doug Kearney happens to be a very good friend of mine, and right at the moment you seem to be what he needs to make him happy. I don't have a problem with that, he doesn't, and neither does his wife. Can I take it you don't, either?"

"No." Stunned, Ryan repeated it to himself. "No, actually, I don't."

But whether this was happening, or whether he had gone quietly out of his mind and was busy hallucinating, Ryan was incapable of deciding. Whatever took place when the President returned would answer that question for him one way or the other, however, and there was little he could do to influence the outcome. And that, in his opinion, was just as it should be, because he had absolutely no idea what, if anything, he actually wanted that outcome to be.

4.

Berry Kearney's birthday party took place at the end of Chad Ryan's fourth week in the White House. Primed by Angela about the kind of gift that would be most appropriate, he turned up bearing a package containing two books – one, purporting to be a technical tome about tennis, contained a lot of pictures of bronzed young men demonstrating their backhands; the other was something to do with the sparkly girl-band sensation even now lip-synching to their own hits in a corner of the East Room. He presented both to Berry with a kiss on the cheek and an expression of good wishes, and looked up from her grinning face to discover the President and First Lady watching with approval a short distance away. He had obviously done something right but was far from sure exactly what.

"Good start." Booth put a glass of champagne into his hand. The room was full of senior staff and their children, some of whom attended school with Berry; the music was jangly, the voices shrill, the clothing bizarre, and Ryan had rarely felt less comfortable in his life.

"Thanks." It was impossible to keep the puzzlement out of his voice.

"What? It's so difficult to accept that they like you? You're going to tell me you're just a guy doing a job and you don't expect anybody to notice? You made yourself conspicuous when you saved his life, Chad; you can't just creep back into your shell and hide now, even if you wanted to. How's it going, anyway?" It was a question he had asked before, but never with the President in the room.

Ryan's eyes sought the dark-clad figure of Kearney before he replied. "Well," he acknowledged.

There had been no repetition of the skinny-dipping incident. In fact, their normal routine – an almost-silent forty-five minutes in the pool every afternoon – had resumed as soon as Kearney got back from South America, but dinner at the Chinese Embassy meant movie night that week had had to be postponed. Ryan had therefore managed to get home at a reasonable hour for once, itself a miracle, and been able to fortify himself for what he was sure would be an ordeal the following afternoon.

"Any new developments?"

"None."

"Like you'd tell me if there were," chuckled Booth. "Nah, that's okay, Chad, I'm not prying. Or if I am, it's because I'm a sad individual and that's the way I get my kicks. Now, I don't want you to worry but it looks as if the First Lady's on her way over here, so I'm going to go get some finger-food and talk to that young lady in the purple sequins. Excuse me."

Opening his mouth to protest, Ryan just managed to turn his anguished expression into a smile of welcome as Kirsten Kearney drew near.

"Colonel Ryan!"

"Ma'am."

"Or may I call you Chad? I gather Doug and Berry already do."

"Please."

"Chad, then. My husband and I are so glad you could join us; I'm afraid Berry's rather smitten with you. I hope that won't be awkward?" Bewilderedly he shook his head. "She liked the gift," continued the First Lady. "I'm assuming that was Angela's choice?"

"It was."

"Good. It's so much simpler when we leave it all to her. Now, Colonel – Chad – if you're agreeable, you could start playing tennis with Berry next week. I think she mentioned that she goes up to Agnes Tack's residence at Arlington? The car leaves the Portico at eight every morning and returns at eleven thirty; could you manage to go with her twice a week, do you think? Tuesdays and Thursdays would be good for us."

"Tuesdays and Thursdays, ma'am, yes. That would be no trouble."

"Also, Angela will let you have the details of my volunteer schedule. I'll be flying out with MSF at the start of next month, probably to Nigeria; wherever people are tempted to steal petroleum from pipelines, there's a constant need for specialist burn treatment."

Chad shuddered. "I envy you the opportunity," he said, unguardedly. Then, realizing how the words could be misinterpreted, hastened to explain. "I mean, you have the chance to see a positive result for the efforts you put in."

"Not always," Kirsten corrected gently. "Sometimes my patients die."

He nodded, thoughtfully. "But sometimes they don't. And you help people with your own hands. That must be very satisfying."

"Hmmm." Glancing around her, the First Lady gripped his arm and steered him to an empty corner of the room between a heavy window-curtain and an ugly plaster bust of Jefferson on a plinth. "Chad, you saved my husband's life. That would be plenty for most people but indirectly you did even more; who knows how many people will have the chance to live the whole of their natural lives simply because Doug wasn't killed that day? Have you ever thought about how different the world would be if Howard Maddocks was President? I guarantee you wouldn't like it very much."

"I don't know him well enough to comment, ma'am," he told her carefully. "And the fact that I don't like him means I wouldn't judge fairly. I have no reason to suppose he wouldn't be a good President."

"Oh, he'd be perfectly adequate," murmured Kirsten. "But he wouldn't be Doug. And while the electorate of this country may have lost faith in my husband, the rest of the world adores him. Ask them some time about seeing a positive result for your efforts."

"Mrs Kearney ... " He had no idea what he wanted to say to her, only that he wanted to make her stop talking. When she did, however, looking at him with the terrifying acuity which her daughter seemed to have inherited in spades, he could only manage to take refuge in platitudes. "Actually, ma'am, I'm quite glad the President is still alive, too."

"I know you are," she grinned. "And one of these days I hope you get a chance to tell him that."

"Kirsten? Chad? You want to let me in on what you two are plotting against me over there?" Kearney was shouldering his way through the gathering – or, rather, teenagers were scattering before him like sheep before by a wolf, re-forming again in a multi-colored spangly tide and apparently taking no notice whatever that the leader of the free world had just sauntered across their dance floor. Berry herself, lost in conversation on the far side of the room, seemed oblivious to his presence. "Can we leave yet?" he asked his wife as he drew level with them.

"Not a chance." A quick glance at the elegant little watch on her left wrist. "At least another half-hour."

"Next year I'm bringing my own booze," Kearney muttered. "We'll have a bottle of something stashed away, Chad, and only you and I will know where it is."

"You'll definitely be here next year, then, Mr President?" Ryan asked, with a wicked twist of his mouth.

Kearney managed something that might have been a smile. "I have contingency plans in place for every possible kind of disaster," he admitted, with a shrug. "I just added that one to the list."

It was very late the same evening, just as Ryan was getting ready for bed, that the telephone rang in his apartment and he snatched it up without thinking. "Yes?"

"It's me," said Kearney.

"It's … Oh God." The voice did a slow burn on him. He had been sleepy and relaxed and his brain had been in neutral, and now all of a sudden none of these things was true. "I'm sorry, yes, of course. Is there … something you need?" He had no idea whether the line was secure or not, or what the nature of the call might be, but he knew better than to use the man's title under any circumstances. If this was a private matter and if there was any doubt about security, the less he said that was identifiable the better.

"You want to meet me at the pool?"

"Now?"

"Yes, now."

Ryan looked down at himself. He was already in his pajama pants and had been about to climb into bed, but he no longer cared about sleep – or anything else, for that matter.

"I'll be a few minutes," he said.

"I'll tell them to expect you."

"Thank you," said Ryan, before the line went dead, and he wondered what he was thanking Kearney for – the invitation? Or the interest?

The short journey had never taken so long before. Although it was past eleven before he set off, the streets were far from deserted and his cab passed through brightly-lighted avenues populated by emerging theater-goers and bar patrons, between restaurants packed with late-night diners, skirting groups of tourists photographing the floodlit landmarks of the city.

By the time he reached the White House, Ryan was struggling to concentrate and failing. His mind was a scattered mess of hopes that he was afraid would be all too visible to anyone he met. There were people in the corridors but he avoided their gazes; he wondered if they would recognize him, dressed in the casual clothes that were the first things he had laid hands on in the rush to be out of the door as quickly as possible. He'd thrown on old chinos, a black tee-shirt and tennis shoes; no underwear, because it seemed to him that whatever he wore he would not be wearing it for long, yet that decision already felt wrong. He had the unnerving sensation that his face was a billboard on which past and future misdeeds were written larger than life, and he could not bear to think that people would see him and know everything – about Kearney, about their intended intimacy – before he had the chance to experience it for himself.

The agents on elevator duty stepped aside to allow him to enter. He barely glanced at them. He stood in the cabin as it descended, rubbing his eyes and pinching the bridge of his nose, trying to get his thoughts into line. This was insane. He was a grown man, tried and seasoned by a military career, not a teenage boy with a crush on some hockey player or gymnast – although that was certainly the way he was feeling at the moment.

If he had been asked a year ago whether there was any man in the world who could make his pulse race, any man for whose company he would risk indignity, disgrace and public exposure, Chad Ryan would have laughed a hollow little laugh and changed the subject; there had never been anybody important enough to court potential disaster for. Back then, though, Douglas Kearney's name had meant nothing but that moderately good-looking political obscurity shoe-horned into the White House to prevent competing factions of his Party tearing each other limb from limb. He'd seemed the best of the worst, that was all; a President nobody could actively dislike simply because he wasn't interesting enough to provoke an extreme response. Now, however, he was something else; now, he was a man with whom to be alone was thrilling in ways he could scarcely begin to comprehend, and to whom he was hurrying like a bride with an overwhelming urgency to be deflowered.

Bennett was in the basement lobby but did not speak as he punched the code to admit Chad, then ceremoniously closed the door again behind him. Chad was grateful for the silence; he knew he could not have opened his mouth without saying something crass or stupid. That nothing had happened to prevent his progress was all the acknowledgement he needed that this thing between himself and Kearney – whatever it was – had allies where it counted. The security sweep and ham-handed fumbling with lighting and ventilation must have all been dealt with before his arrival, because once inside the pool complex it was obvious he had the place to himself. It was just him, the quiet lapping of the water, the bundle of towels placed ready on the bench.

Towels.

That was everything he needed to know, right there. Clothing of any sort would obviously be superfluous.

He tried to imagine where the President might be. There had been something at the Kennedy Center, although he could not remember what – chamber music of some sort, he recollected vaguely. He pictured the brief journey back to the White House, the motorcade sweeping along empty roads with nothing to impede its progress. The limousine would glide into the shelter of the Portico and Kearney would disembark and step into the building surrounded by staff. Had the First Lady been scheduled to attend the event this evening? He had no idea. Perhaps she would kiss him on the cheek, wish him well, and set off to the Residence to sleep. Tired-eyed aides would stumble away to write up their notes; others would drop by their desks to collect messages, or pick up cabs to head off to the suburbs, to wives and children. As long as no national emergency supervened, the President would soon be as alone as he ever got, striding through the silent halls with his agents at his side.

They would know where he was going, of course, and they would know, or at least guess, why.

Right now, the entire machinery of the Presidency was focused on putting himself and Douglas Kearney into a room together, so that they could find out what might happen between them. Although, he supposed, none of them was in any more doubt about that than he was himself.

Chad stepped out of his clothes and piled them, as he usually did, tidily. He did not look in the mirror; whatever Kearney saw in him was obviously something he was incapable of seeing in himself. The only concession he made to appearance was the automatic brush of one hand through his hair – a gesture negated when, a moment later, he ran lightly across the textured tile, bent at the knees, and sprang easily into the water. It was a perfect dive. He caught himself wishing Kearney had been there to see it; he could picture his expression of amused admiration, the elder-brotherly fondness amounting almost to pride, the smart-mouthed but affectionate comment he would have made.

Pushing to the bottom of the pool, he let his knuckles scrape across its ridged floor before he kicked up again. He felt pampered and indulged in this most secret of spaces; water flowed across him, teasing and sensitizing his body, droplets stroking through his hair and eyelashes and running in rivers over the planes and hollows of his chest. It was tactile but elusive, warm and cold at the same time, obvious and ambiguous and, like his relationship with Kearney, he could not fully grasp it but knew it was something he could not hope to exist without. Then he lay on his back, floating, wondering what it would be like to be held in the darkness of a sensory deprivation tank, letting his mind free associate beyond its normal boundaries. It would be surreal, a psychedelic journey, the kind of out-of-body experience that usually involved some kind of chemical stimulus; the kind, in fact, on which he was presently embarked without benefit of any drug stronger than his feelings for the President. Wild as it may have seemed, he was getting higher on knowledge and acceptance of his desire for the man than he had ever been before; it was becoming abundantly clear to him that Douglas Kearney was his drug of choice, his addiction, his necessity, and it was a condition for which there was no readily apparent cure.

This ecstatic reverie lasted only a short while before the sounds of the elevator became audible through the basement wall. He heard the cabin arrive and its doors open, and the click of the lock on the changing room door. After that, there was silence. Chad ducked his head below the surface of the water, eyes open, mind calm, and rose serene and ready for whatever was to follow.

Beyond his line of sight there was a cacophony of swearing, hurry, elephantine slamming-about and wrestling with clothing. It took him by surprise; haste and imprecision were not conditions he normally associated with Kearney, whose public persona, if a little unfinished, was urbane and effective. That he was capable of being anything less than entirely stylish came as quite a shock.

A moment later, he appeared in the doorway. Somewhere along the way he had disposed of his watch, jacket, shoes, underwear and trousers; now he was hauling open a crisp bow-tie and letting it fall to the floor. He was, however, fighting a losing battle with his shirt; most of its buttons had been wrestled loose and one had snapped and fallen with an impatient sound. One cuff-link followed, dropping with the chink of a golden coin. The second, however, would not be moved. Kearney continued to wrangle with it, standing naked but for an open evening shirt that had once been starched and white as a snow-bank but now hung from his shoulders like a limp rag.

He cursed at the shirt, the link, the world and all its creations.

Then he turned slowly to look at Chad, eyes glittering and acquisitive – and dived in, shirt and all. In two or three long, fierce strokes he had pulled himself through the water and solidly into his arms.

"My God, man," he gasped. "I thought we'd never get to this point! For a while there I really wondered if I was going to have to hire a sky-writer!"

Chad clutched at him, too stunned to reply, overwhelmed by the living strength pressed against him. He had not realized how much he missed this kind of thing; the closeness, the sensations of touch and taste and smell. Kearney was just that much taller, broader and stronger than himself for him to feel surrounded, protected and shielded from every disaster; he leaned into the warmth, let it enfold him, yielding to the luxury of being held, letting his hands stroke across the muscular back and shoulders and press the man tighter and tighter to him until he thought neither of them would ever breathe again.

When he managed to reassemble himself sufficiently to speak, the sound of his own voice terrified him.

"Doug?" he whispered, nervously.

Close to his ear a deep voice said, "It's okay, don't be scared."

"I was sure I was going mad."

"So was I."

The confusion of wet hands on wet skin resolved itself somehow into square palms framing Chad's face, into lips that fastened eagerly on his own; breathless, unsettled little kisses at first, tentative bird-pecks still unsure of their welcome despite every evidence of alacrity, then settling to scorching intensity and depth. He was swept into Kearney's arms, Fay Wray melded against King Kong, losing himself in the possessive mouth. It had been rare in Chad's acquaintance that men actually kissed their partners, but one who kissed like this – utterly involved and absorbed in the experience – was without exemplar. Memories of those others were completely swept away in a heartbeat; they had been dilettantes, failed facsimiles of men who had taken their mechanical pleasure and moved on. There was more emotion here and now, between himself and Kearney, than he had ever shared with a lover before, and it was both glorious and tragic to have to admit it.

"You must have known." Lips and teeth on his neck, grazing and nipping hungrily at his skin.

"I didn't, I swear I didn't. Perhaps I wouldn't let myself think about it. It didn't seem remotely possible."

Hands on Chad's backside pulled their bodies together, fiercely aroused and hot and slick where they caught and rubbed. "Not possible I'd want you?"

"You're the President." Feeling dizzy and unconnected, he said it as if it explained everything.

"No, I'm not. I've been trying to tell you, Ryan; you're not with the President, you're with me. I'm not that guy."

"I'm sorry. It took me a while." Chad's hands slid under the button band of Kearney's dress shirt and strolled idly across his chest. It was an intimacy he had dreamed of and reality did not disappoint. His tingling fingertips reveled in the textures of soft skin, scattered curls, the sharp little knots of nipples. He kissed water-diamonds from Kearney's neck and the dripping ends of his hair. "I get it now."

"It's a shell," Kearney went on. "It's a suit I wear. I'm not a king, I wasn't born to this, I don't have to stay with it from cradle to grave. It's eight years at the most, and I'm nearly half-way through it already. And if you knew how much I didn't want to be President in the first place ..."

"Hush." He stroked a hand through Kearney's hair, soft pepper-and-salt strands which caught the muted light in a variety of ways.

"Please, please, just let me be not-the-President for a while with you. I swear, when you're around, the world could go to hell for all the notice I take. If you knew about all the meetings I've screwed up because I can't get my mind off you, if you knew about the things I want to do with you that I haven't done with anybody else in half a lifetime ... Chad, sometimes you make me so damned horny I can't even remember my own name."

"I do?"

"God, yes. I could never figure out Kennedy – why he'd risk everything for women, I mean. Don't get me wrong, Marilyn Monroe would have tempted a saint – which he wasn't, and neither am I. But I never understood why he couldn't keep it in his pants, you know? Only this job is ... You get confused, and people don't say what they mean, and you get exhausted and you want someone who'll make it simple, someone who's prepared to ... "

"Adore you?"

Kearney looked away. "You say that as if it was a bad thing."

"It isn't. Not at all." And, incongruous as it was to be wanted to the point of distraction, he could almost understand it. There must be more worthy men in the world, more appropriate objects for a President's lust – handsome, heroic men who would ornament any administration – but maybe men like that had egos to match their talents. Maybe what a lion needed, more than anything else, was the undemanding company of a mouse. It otherwise defied belief that any man could be overwhelmed with desire for a middle-aged nobody of modest looks, negligible achievements and absolutely no ambition; it was almost bizarre. "You shouldn't worry about it."

"I know. But it started the moment you walked into my life, and now I can't think about anything else. And you'd better want me too, because I'm just about at breaking-point here."

"Oh yes," Chad told him, although no such assurance was necessary. He had thought it was self-evident but when the hot whisper across Kearney's ear drew a groan of desperation, it became apparent that the man had been waiting for some sort of formal confirmation of interest from him. "I do want you. Of course I do."

His hands were shaking. Somehow he managed to make his fingers fasten on the gold nub of the remaining cuff-link and push it through the sodden shirt cuff. Then he peeled away Kearney's shirt and set it afloat on the surface of the water like a wet white cloud. It bore up for a second or two until its fibers became completely saturated, then it slid gracefully out of sight.

Chad held the cuff-link into the light, turning it one way and another, examining the reflections that it cast. When he let it fall from his fingers he watched it drifting slowly down through the water.

"We shouldn't do this here," Kearney told him. "It involves too many other people. But I want to be alone with you and I just don't know where else we can go. Would it be possible to secure your apartment somehow, do you think?"

Chad's head swam. "I doubt it. I don't think it would be easy, and it's much too dangerous for you anyway. If you were caught ... "

"That's the problem. I could disguise myself as a delivery guy or something, but one wide-awake neighbor is all you need and suddenly it's a scandal." Nevertheless his large hand was making free of Chad's wet flank, and his words were sanity punctuated by the madness of kisses. Whatever effort at discipline he was making was being overwhelmed by the powerful forces of arousal. "Anyway, you deserve better than that.

You deserve better than this." Yet he walked Chad back against the side of the pool, hitched him so that he was half-perched on the grab-rail. Chad spread his thighs to accommodate Kearney, drawing him in, locking feet around his hips and arms around his neck and relaxing deliberately, held by a grip that he could have broken with a word. There were hands beneath him, supporting him, the mouth breathless against his skin, the frictionless friction of groin against groin and the dragging of hot flesh and cool water in unpredictable oppositions.

"I don't really care," he whispered. "Here and now is fine with me, Doug. Anything else … "

"What?"

"I don't care about anything else," he repeated. "Here and now is all there is."

It began slowly at first, small movements, delicate touches, wet sliding thrusts between tight-packed abdomens, fingernails digging half-moons into Kearney's biceps and Chad's taut backside. It was random, open-mouthed, the product of need and inability to reason, groaning with the obscenity of frustrated lust. Logical facilities suspended, they were simply mouths and bodies responding to one another without thought, seeking atavistic satisfaction as fundamental as the need for air. Kearney, who for years had denied himself this particular pleasure, was on a collision course with himself; the halves of his divided personality, which craved socially acceptable and unacceptable company, were rushing back together, reforming, reacting, meshing and melding to recreate a coherent unity.

And it was far too urgent to last; Chad slipped over the brink into helpless orgasm, cresting and leaving him pliant with Kearney still hard between his thighs, clawing towards relief, ultimately collapsing into a breathless wreck of blissed-out anguish.

"My god," Chad whispered, after a long interval. They were sweating, loose-limbed, incapable of thought. He was stroking the back of Kearney's neck, his fingers making the smallest but most possessive of movements, his eyes closed, his body draped languidly in supportive arms. He had no desire to be awakened from this moment, no intention of facing reality until it was absolutely and irrevocably necessary to do so. "That was good."

"Did I hurt you?"

"No, but I wouldn't have minded if you had."

Kearney kissed him absent-mindedly. "Thank you."

"Hush. You know you're more than welcome."

"I'm not usually … such an animal, I guess."

"It's okay. Sometimes that's what it takes."

"Yeah. But I'd been hoping we could make it last a little while longer. Enjoy it properly. Do it somewhere … damn it, somewhere with a bed, at least!"

"We will," Chad assured him, tenderly. "Next time."

Kearney leaned in and found his wet mouth; his tongue moving to explore lips, teeth, the throat that hollowed to receive it. "Damn, your mouth's good. I really, really hope you like to suck cock."

"I used to," he grinned. "It's been a while; I'll see if I can remember how it works – provided I can do it without drowning, of course."

"And getting fucked? You like that, too?"

"Doesn't everyone?"

Kearney's body relaxed further. "Yes, everyone does." Then, after a pause, "You understand, Chad? Everyone does."

"Including you? I understand."

The last of the tension slipped from Kearney's shoulders, falling away through the water as irrevocably as the discarded shirt.

"You can't imagine how much I'm going to need you, Chad. There's no way I'll get through a second term without this. I thought I'd got it all out of my system ages ago – I didn't think about it for years and years and I honestly thought I'd outgrown it, but it came back. Right in the middle of the campaign, when it was too late to back out, I suddenly started having dreams about men again. Just really hot, sexy dreams about hands, bodies, mouths. You can imagine how I felt; I thought that part of my life was over for good."

"Yes."

"Kirsten thinks it's to do with stress, but that doesn't make it go away – and when you're elected to office the stress goes on getting worse. So we made a deal – I stayed in the campaign, but we agreed that if a guy ever came along that we both felt safe with ... she wouldn't try to stop it happening. And the dumb part is, the moment I saw you on television after you saved my life I started thinking maybe you could be the guy."

"Why?" Chad asked, bewildered. "Whatever did you see in me?"

"I don't know. You were just being yourself, I guess. You weren't someone with an agenda, you weren't gray, you weren't dull, you weren't trying to prove a point. You were who you are, and I liked you for that."

"Thank you." Chad caressed the weathered jawline with the tips of his fingers, reveling in the fact that – briefly – he had license to do so.

"We could be a really good team," Kearney went on softly. "I'm not going to make any extravagant promises, except that I'll try to make sure you never regret a moment. If you could ... be with me for a little while, help me get through the next four years ... you could probably save my sanity, and a lot of people would be grateful – including me. Stay with me, Chad? Please?"

"You ... " he faltered, looking up, "you don't have to worry. I'm here because I want to be here; I had plenty of opportunities to back away and I didn't choose to take any of them. If we can make each other happy, I'm sure we can cope with whatever the world throws at us. I'm coming along for the ride, Doug. If ever you want rid of me, you're going to have to say so in words so simple that even I can understand them."

"I don't want rid of you, honey." The unthinking endearment was both surprising and somehow exactly suitable. "I want you to stay. One of these days, I believe you and I could have something absolutely extraordinary together."

"I think, Mr President," said Chad, his lips just brushing the lobe of Kearney's ear and his warm breath stroking softly inside it, "if you examine the situation, you'll probably find that we have something absolutely extraordinary together already."

5.

It was late that night before they managed to tear themselves apart, and even then it was only with the greatest possible reluctance and because, after a while, the swimming pool no longer offered the most comfortable or welcoming ambiance for a tryst. They lingered as long as they could under a warm shower, their pretense at soaping and washing only the merest veneer of an excuse for slow, languorous exploration of one another's bodies punctuated by the exchange of kisses and the sort of idle remarks best left unrecorded. Eventually, however, it became necessary to separate for the night.

Kearney left first, under pressure to get at least a couple of hours' sleep before a scheduled conference call with the Greek Prime Minister, escorted into the elevator by one of Bennett's colleagues. A few minutes, later Ryan walked out to the Portico with Bennett beside him, and was seated in the back of a cab and taken home swiftly through what was now early morning. He was tired but elated, his body thrumming from Kearney's touch, torn between wanting rest and wanting more. He could still feel the President's caresses, and the scent of the President's skin was on the palms of his hands. They had learned one another very thoroughly in the past few hours and any remaining barriers of modesty between them had been completely demolished. There was nothing about one another now that they felt they did not know.

And yet it had ended too soon and the world had intervened between them. Nothing was ready, there was no bedroom to which they could retreat to finish out the night together, and they parted in a strange hybrid mood balanced between exhilaration and yearning. Ryan did not know whether he could quite believe Kearney's casual "I'll call you," as he stepped into the elevator. Of course Kearney intended to do what he promised, but there would always be things to take his attention away from this elusive little mirage of an affair. Ryan could scarcely bring himself to believe that he held any great significance in the man's life, whatever Kearney might say. Yet it was satisfying to drift to sleep almost as the sun was finding the city and to float in dreams through visions of their time together, of what had been and of what might yet come to be.

The next time his telephone rang he knew who it was. He was still in bed, and he lifted the receiver slowly and said, "Hi."

"Hi yourself," was the quiet answer. "How are you?"

"Good. Better than good. Phenomenal."

"Yup, me too." And then there was silence for a long time. "You're sure this is what you want?" asked Kearney at last.

"It is – as long as it's what you want, too."

"Yes. But you understand people are going to have to know? If you're absolutely sure, then I'm going to start talking to a few folks."

"The first one being … ?" The implication was obvious.

"I already told her. Not that I needed to. She knew as soon as she set eyes on me."

"Oh."

"Think I'm probably going to get a reputation for smiling at people today." A little chuckle, almost forced.

"I'm glad." Ryan relaxed back against his pillows and concentrated on the disembodied voice. "I miss you."

At the other end of the line Kearney groaned. "There aren't going to be many more chances like that," he said. "We need to figure out some alternatives."

"Okay. You know I'll … I mean, whatever's good for you."

"Okay. So, I should probably do some work. Were you sleeping?"

"Yes. Well, drowsing."

"Sounds great. I wish I could."

"You deserve to."

"Well, I'll catch up." And extreme reluctance to ring off registered in every syllable. "Can I call you again?"

"Of course. Not too often, though."

"I know. Maybe tomorrow?"

"That would be good," whispered Ryan, and for a moment the thought hung in the silence between them. Then the line went dead without any 'goodbyes', and he knew that it was something they were never really going to say again.

Monday was mayhem, albeit of the subdued and seething variety. Coming through security into the Northwest Lobby at his regular time, Ryan was startled to be greeted by Joel Cooledge looking thinner in the face and more pensive than ever. There was a distinct absence of friendliness in the agent's manner this morning, which was an immediate cause for concern; it was apparent that something had gone wrong and that tempers were barely being suppressed.

"Colonel." Only the most perfunctory greeting. "Mr Booth needs you in the Oval Office right away."

"Has something happened?"

"I don't know the details. I believe it's something to do with improper use of a White House facility."

Ryan stopped in his tracks and stared at Cooledge in disbelief. "The pool?" he asked.

"It would seem so, sir." The tone of the agent's voice had become almost sympathetic. "The Vice President's already here," he added.

"Damn. Is there going to be trouble?"

"Yes, Colonel, there is. I'm sorry."

They marched side by side along the corridor, taking very little notice of their surroundings. Entering the outer precincts of the Oval Office it became obvious that all was not well; Mitchell Booth was in gray-faced colloquy with a member of the secretarial team, and they both looked around as Ryan entered. Cooledge nodded briskly and made himself scarce, discretion apparently still being the better part of valor, even for a fully trained member of the Secret Service.

"Thank God you're here," Booth muttered, stepping across and gripping Ryan's arm. "You're probably the only person apart from the First Lady who could calm him down, and we're not planning to involve her in this unless we absolutely have to."

"In what? Joel didn't seem to know what the problem was."

Booth drew him to one side and lowered his voice further. "Mike Bennett is usually the Vice President's agent. They're buddies;

Maddocks knew Bennett's father about a hundred years ago. Some time over the weekend, Bennett told Maddocks about what happened in the pool Friday night. You guys really need to learn the word 'discretion', Chad."

"He ... told him?"

"He'd have had to know about it sooner or later anyway," Booth said, reasonably. "You're living in a goldfish bowl now; the President doesn't take a dump without somebody or other wanting details. Bennett probably assumed the VP already knew about the relationship. Whether he did or not, he's pretty mad the President didn't tell him personally. You're going to have to go in there right away; Doug said to send you in the moment you arrived."

"Oh."

"Yeah. Guess this is when you find out exactly how much this guy's worth to you, isn't it?"

Ryan looked at him levelly. "I already know," he said.

"Good man. Try to stay calm and let's see if we can get Doug's blood-pressure back below the red line, shall we? And don't worry, help's on its way." So saying, he steered Chad over to the wide doorway and left him there, squaring his shoulders as if he was going on parade. It was a sickening moment, not unlike the last few seconds before a parachute drop; it really didn't matter how much training one had received, there were some situations that were just flat out impossible to predict.

Ryan listened for a moment. However thick the door, however good the sound proofing, a Chief Executive in a foul mood and making no attempt to be quiet could be heard over a large proportion of the White House.

"You have no right to involve Government staff in your sordid sexual dalliances," Maddocks was saying loudly, as if he really thought he could shout the President down.

"This house is not a prison," Kearney told him, a bitter edge to his voice. "I earn my free time and how I choose to spend it is my affair."

"Not when you risk making this country ridiculous in the eyes of the world. Do you have any idea how some of the more conservative nations we deal with would react if it got out? They hate you already; they'd be burning you in effigy if they knew about this!"

"Oh yeah? And you're going to be the one who tells them, are you?"

"'Sources close to the White House.'"

"Some sources may not be close to the White House for a hell of a lot longer," Kearney told him coldly.

"Yeah? And who gets my job? Chad? We'll be knee deep in Declarations of War by the end of the week."

Ryan opened the door and slipped in quietly, closing it behind him with a click. Kearney was on his feet behind his desk, dressed in his usual smart dark suit, crisp white shirt and soberly-colored tie. Above the line of his collar a fading bite mark was still just visible on his neck. Facing him, with only the desk preventing them from tearing one another limb from limb, was the Vice President, his ominous manner eloquent of brooding and ill-contained aggression.

Distracted, Kearney flicked a quick glance in Ryan's direction and the set of his face softened momentarily.

"Chad."

"Mr President." Slightly tentative, he took a few steps forward. "Mr Vice President."

"Get out," Maddocks snapped in response. "I'm not having this conversation with him present."

"This is not a conversation, it's an argument. It concerns him. He stays."

"I don't believe this!" Maddocks seethed. "In all my years of public service I've never met a President who insisted on discussing matters of policy in front of the help! For God's sake, Doug, stop letting your dick make decisions for you. If you must fuck him, don't do it in a Government facility. Keep your private life separate from your public duty. Other Presidents were happy enough to play it that way, why can't you?"

"I'm not other Presidents."

"No, you're not," Maddocks told him, meeting him in the same sub-Arctic register. "Because out of all the crooks, clowns and lunatics who had this office before you, there has never yet been one irresponsible enough to let himself get caught screwing anybody in an unsecured location."

"It was secured! There were agents on the door!"

"Agents who should never ever have known what you were doing," was the grim-faced response. "You put my guy in an untenable position, Doug. It was all I could do to stop him resigning. You can't just assume revoking 'Don't ask, Don't tell' will make everybody pro-gay. You've got to remember there's a strong Christian right in this country and not everyone shares your enthusiasm for alternative lifestyles. If you're determined to commit political suicide, go ahead and do it by all means but I'm damned if I'll let you take me and the rest of this administration with you. We all worked far too hard to get here in the first place. I'm not going to see it thrown away for the sake of some ... " He stopped, looked Ryan up and down with the censorious expression of a pest exterminator wondering which brand of rodenticide to use. "Let's face it," he said, devastatingly, "some cheap cocksucker."

"That's enough!" seethed Kearney. "One more word and I'll bust your ass so far you'll be glad of a job counting paper-clips in a bomb shelter in Arkansas!"

"You can keep your goddamn' queer hands away from my ass," was the brutal response. "Get rid of him, Doug. You're not a private citizen any more, you can't just take a holiday from the Presidency whenever you feel like it. Whoever a President fucks it has national security implications, and if you're so besotted you can't see that ... well, maybe you just shouldn't be the President any more."

"I'll have your resignation on my desk by noon." The fury had gone from Kearney's expression, to be replaced by the sickening recognition of inevitability.

"Sure you will, if that's what you really want. But think about what you're throwing away here. Think about the confidence of the American people – the people who voted for you. Don't compromise their love and respect for the sake of a piece of ass, however cute you may happen to think it is." Maddocks's expression made it abundantly clear that he could not imagine what anyone, his President least of all, could see in a sad-eyed, slightly shop-worn article like Chad Ryan. He was no oil painting, no Adonis, not even a muscular stud. "Air Force Colonels are two for a quarter around this city; Ryan may mean a lot to you, Mr President, but is he really worth giving up everything you've worked for all your life?"

Maddocks paused, looking from one to the other of the two men he had criticized so roundly. Kearney's face was stone, his gaze cold and unyielding, his mouth set into a thin, bitter line. Ryan watched him in bewilderment; understanding for the first time exactly what Kearney had risked for that brief carefree time alone with him was even more of a shock than the knowledge that Kearney had wanted him in the first place.

"I'll go write out my resignation," Maddocks conceded, his anger moderating to a more manageable level. "If you change your mind, Mr President, let me know any time within the next ... four hours ... and I'll tear it up and throw it away. But we'll have to come to some kind of rational agreement about the Colonel here, because I refuse to allow you to compromise your dignity or that of this country with any more bone-headed escapades like this one. I trust I make myself clear?"

With this peroration he turned and made his way out of the room, and the chasm left by his departure was suddenly wider than the Grand Canyon.

After he had gone it was a long time before Kearney would meet Ryan's enquiring gaze. When he did he said nothing, just held out his arms, and a moment later Ryan was in them, hugging him as tightly as he knew how, crushing thousands of dollars worth of exclusive tailoring as he buried his face against Kearney's neck.

"I screwed up," Kearney muttered into his hair. "God, I really screwed up. I forgot that the Presidency shows up every little flaw magnified a million times."

"You telling me you're not perfect?"

"I'm not."

"Big surprise," Ryan whispered. "How do we get out of this one, Doug?"

"Let him stew for a while, then climb down and ask him to stay," was the weary response. "He's right, it was stupid. Beyond stupid. The dumbest, most irresponsible thing any President has ever done."

"Bay of Pigs stupid? Vietnam stupid? Watergate stupid?"

"Worse than any of those. I wanted you so much, I let it affect my judgment. He's right, I was thinking with my dick. Maybe I should just resign and let him finish out my term after all."

"You can't!"

"Oh no? Watch me."

"No more stupid risks, Doug. Please."

"No more stupid risks. But God, wasn't it worth it? I love the way we are together. I love everything about this relationship."

Exuberantly he bent his head, pulled Ryan back into his arms, let their mouths move together into a deep kiss of perfect equality so all-encompassing that even the sound of the door opening and closing again was not enough to drive them apart. It barely registered with either set of senses, in fact, and neither man could spare enough intellectual capacity to analyze or process the implications of the sound.

A door had opened. They had been seen.

It scarcely seemed to matter, and as the kiss ended they stood forehead to forehead, giving and receiving moral support, not caring that there might be anyone else in the room with them until a gentle voice broke through their idyll.

"So, Doug, Chad," Kirsten Kearney said brightly, "why don't you fill me in on what I've missed?"

"He pulled rank, got himself bumped up to first meeting of the day," Kearney finished, a short time later. "I was at my desk by six and he was here at a quarter after. We've been arguing about it ever since." He glanced around his small audience briefly. Kirsten and Ryan, side by side, were drinking coffee laced with brandy. Booth, propped in an armchair, was drinking brandy to which a little coffee had been added. It was early in the day for alcohol, but somehow they all felt they had earned it.

"Bennett's always worked for Maddocks. Apparently, they met yesterday and immediately afterwards Howard started questioning the housekeeping staff about out of hours use of the pool complex. We

68

couldn't expect them to lie for us." An uncomfortable shrug, indicating the hopelessness of the situation. "He waited until he was sure of his facts, then he demanded to see me first thing this morning. Well, you saw what he was like."

"What's his problem?" Ryan asked. "Homophobia?"

"I don't think so. He's never really liked me, but I think it's more than that. I guess I'm just too much of a maverick for him generally."

"And he's in a stronger position in the polls than you are at the moment," Booth commented. "Think he's going to use this to launch his own campaign for November?"

"Could be that," Kearney responded. "Although I'm not sure he'd have challenged me about it if that was what he was planning. Wouldn't he just have kept it to himself and tried to use it against me at a later stage?"

"Probably. The point is, he doesn't know how to deal with a strong President who makes his own decisions; he's used to working with puppets, and he doesn't like you because he can't manipulate you behind the scenes. Maybe it would have suited him better if Chad hadn't actually saved your life that day."

"Are you suggesting my Vice President wants me dead?" Kearney was appalled.

"Not in so many words. But I can see how he could have turned it to his advantage if you'd been killed – and you can bet he saw it at the time, too. He'd have bullied Congress until it started doing things his way. He'd have set this country back ten years or more and then we'd have needed another Douglas Kearney to drag us back into the twenty first century."

"But I stayed alive and thwarted his ambitions. No wonder he's focusing all his frustration and disappointment on you, Chad; saving me put a crimp in his career. Every time he sees us together, it reminds him what he's lost out on."

"So send me away," Ryan suggested, evenly. "Give me a job to do in Alaska or New Mexico or somewhere. I don't want to be caught up in any kind of tactical battle between you and Maddocks. You need him far more than you need me!"

Kearney glared at him. "Oh yeah? Remind me again, Chad, where was he standing when Corrado came after me with a gun? How many bullets did he take for my sake? When you were with me in the pool, where was he? Out here, plotting against us both! If I have to make a choice," he underlined, setting the matter to rest for what he clearly hoped would be the last time, "I'd rather keep you and find myself a new Vice President."

"I thought you wanted him inside the tent pissing out rather than outside pissing in?" Ryan asked, in some bewilderment.

"Given a choice, I'd rather not have him pissing at all," was the fervent response. "But if he does, it won't be all over you."

"Thank you for that vivid image, Mr President," Mitch said, coolly. "Chad, if this thing ever hits the press, everybody's gonna know who you are. So much for staying out of the limelight."

"Then we'd better make sure it doesn't hit," Kearney put in, firmly. "Much as it pains me, I'm going to have to get Howard back in here, apologize to him in front of all three of you, and ask him not to resign. Hopefully he agrees, and then we join forces and try to concentrate on damage limitation. I will not allow this administration to disintegrate in scandal and lies," he completed, his expression grim. "I'd rather walk away."

"Sit down, Howard."

Half an hour later, under the scrutiny of three pairs of critical eyes, this was a meeting of wild animals who faced one another uneasily. Maddocks obeyed.

"I owe you an apology." Forestalling the unheard response with a wave of the hand, Kearney continued unimpeded. "Yes, the country too. But you were the one I lost my temper with. I was wrong and I didn't want to hear it. I deserved everything you said to me. I'd like you to stay on as Vice President; you'd be virtually impossible to replace."

Maddocks looked slowly around the room, contemplating his reply. "What happens about Colonel Ryan?"

"He stays. Chad's place in my life is non-negotiable."

Maddocks glanced up quickly, meeting Kirsten Kearney's calm gaze.

"You're in agreement with this?"

"Chad is our family's friend, Howard, not just Doug's. Every one of us loves him dearly, and we don't want to part with him. But we're willing to de-emphasize his friendship with the President, if that's what it takes to keep you with us."

Maddocks did not respond directly to the First Lady's words, but returned his attention to Kearney. "No more unscheduled or inappropriate use of White House facilities," he stipulated, brusquely. "If there's some reason not to use the Residence, we have houses and apartments all over the city; any one of them can be made available to you whenever you like. And don't even consider Ryan's apartment; I've had my guys inside there and it leaks like a sieve. Hell, I'd rather you took him to Camp David if you absolutely have to; at least those guys up there are used to hiding stuff away. But, trust me, if you take one more stupid risk over this guy, you'll find his picture alongside yours on every front page in the entire English-speaking world."

A sharp intake of breath in the room. This was undoubtedly blackmail, but at least it was openly stated and understood by all parties; there was nothing there that would compromise what remained of the President's integrity. Kearney stared down the incipient protest, then nodded towards Maddocks.

"Okay," he said, "I deserve that. I'm not going to try to wriggle out of it." A humiliating capitulation, but only for the sake of a greater victory to come.

"Good. Then with your permission, Mr President, I'll rip up my letter of resignation and we'll say no more about it." Maddocks put a hand inside his jacket, drew out a white envelope and held it poised. At a confirmatory nod from Kearney he ripped the envelope in two, then in two again, and let the pieces fall onto the polished surface of the coffee table. Whether his letter of resignation had in fact been inside the envelope or not, it was a strongly symbolic gesture.

"Thank you, Howard."

"Thank you, Mr President." Getting to his feet, Maddocks accepted a rather shamefaced handshake. "I'm sorry it had to come to this."

"So am I."

Maddocks stepped away and found himself facing the Air Force officer at the epicenter of the argument.

"Ryan." He offered his hand, and Ryan did not hesitate to take it. "Nothing personal," the Vice President said. "I don't know you. I shouldn't have called you a cocksucker."

Ryan shrugged. "Technically, sir, it's perfectly accurate," he allowed, with complete composure, "although I certainly wouldn't describe myself as cheap."

The look on Maddocks's face at this remark – appalled, astounded, more than a little embarrassed – was one the others in the room would cherish for the rest of their lives.

"We should have been more discreet," Ryan added, consolingly.

"You should. If there's nothing else, Mr President?" Kearney shook his head. "Then excuse me, I have work to do. Kirsten. Booth." Brief nods of acknowledgement all round, and Howard Maddocks strode away from the Oval Office leaving an impressive silence behind him.

"'Technically it's perfectly accurate'?" Kearney repeated, when he felt sufficient time had elapsed. "You've never thought about going into politics, have you, Chad?"

"No, I haven't. Do you think I should?"

"No!" Three voices in unison, and then a dissolution into uneasy laughter.

"We got away with it, didn't we?" Kirsten asked.

"This time," her husband confirmed. "I'm glad it happened, though, and I'm glad it wasn't worse. We'll just have to be a hell of a lot more careful in the future. Chad, you might want to get a list of those properties Howard mentioned and take a look at some of them. Think about getting rid of your apartment and moving in here. Put your stuff into storage and I'll pay."

"Okay." The usual no-quibble decisive response.

"Kirsten, I … "

"We'll talk about it later," the First Lady said, firmly. "Don't you people have any work to do today? Or is the country running itself?"

"I think it's running itself," Booth smiled. "It couldn't be doing a worse job than we are, that's for sure. Mr President, you have a defense strategy meeting in thirty minutes and I don't believe you've read the briefing document."

"Excuse me," Ryan said, turning for the door, "I missed breakfast."

"So did I!" Kirsten exclaimed, taking his arm and escorting him towards the exit. "Come along, Chad, let's see if we can't get someone to make us some waffles!"

Shortly afterwards they were sitting at a sunlit table by a window in the White House Residence, finishing breakfast, their nerves considerably calmer than they had been an hour before.

"Mitch sent Olivia to find me," Kirsten supplied, thoughtfully. "He figured Howard probably didn't realize I knew; I suspect at least part of his plan involved threatening to out you guys to me. He back-pedaled on that pretty quickly, if it was what he had in mind."

"He assured me he wasn't going to involve you," Ryan protested mildly.

"He lied. Mitch is under strict instructions to have me fetched if there's ever anything of the sort. Did you really imagine I wouldn't want to be there to support my husband and his friend when they needed me?"

"All the same, I'm sorry we embarrassed you."

"You didn't. I know where all of Doug's bodies are buried, Chad, believe me. You don't go into a Presidential campaign without having some pretty uninhibited conversations first, and Doug's been on the fence about his sexuality ever since I've known him. Although," she added, with a smile, "I think he could be on the verge of making a decision at last, and I must admit I'd be relieved. It's always been a struggle, trying to reconcile the tough image people have of him with the knowledge that underneath it all he's probably more gay than straight. We've both known for a while that one day there would be 'a guy', although we couldn't imagine who he'd be or what he'd be like. You must know Doug's pretty smitten with you, Chad? In fact, if we're not all extremely careful, he could well end up falling head over heels in love."

Embarrassed, Ryan turned away. "I doubt it."

"Why not? You think just because he's who he is that he doesn't have the same kind of weaknesses as everybody else? Do you have any idea how many Presidents have had affairs while they were in office?" She let the question hang for a moment, then answered it herself. "Most of them."

"I know that. But I'm not the kind of person people fall in love with. Let's be honest, I'm not exactly Marilyn Monroe – am I?"

"I should hope not, poor woman. You don't imagine Doug would deal with you as unkindly as Kennedy did with her, do you?"

"No, of course not. But I'm ... "

"Older and more cynical? Not as cute in a gown?" Kirsten teased. "Lighten up, Chad. You want him, don't you? Don't try to pretend you don't."

"Mrs Kearney! How am I supposed to answer that? It's a closed question."

"'Mrs Kearney?'" she repeated, gently. "Try to remember that my name is 'Kirsten'. And you don't really need to answer; the way you stood up with him against Maddocks was an answer in itself. You love him, don't you?"

The quietly insistent tone of a confessor broke through his limited attempts at defense. He leaned forward, hand over his eyes, and she saw rather than heard his lips form the answer. "Yes."

"Then he'll move Heaven and Earth to get what he wants," she whispered, putting a hand on his shoulder. "Haven't you learned that about him by now?"

"Yes, of course. But how could I ever imagine that I ... "

" ... would be what he wanted?" she finished for him. "I understand that." She paused, then started again on a different tack. "Tell me something, Chad. Tell me what you want out of the relationship. I don't suppose anybody's got around to asking you that yet, have they?"

"Ha!" He gave a cynical little laugh and met her gaze levelly, but she could see hurt in his eyes. "What does anybody want in a relationship? Marriage. A split-level three-bedroom in a select neighborhood, two children and a dog. Two cars in the garage, country club membership, a husband who comes home every day at five o'clock and never so much as looks at another Colonel."

Kirsten's smile grew warmer. If he were still strong enough to joke about this, there was every chance he could survive without being overwhelmed.

"You, Chad," she soothed. "Not Marilyn Monroe. What do you want?"

He sat back in the seat, looking considerably older than his years. "How can I tell you when I don't even know myself?" He stopped. "A man, I suppose. What I don't want, Kirsten, is someone else's husband. Or a President, if it comes to that."

"Unfortunately they're part of the deal," the First Lady reminded him. "At least for a while. As long as he's in office, you'll just have to take him as he is – job, wife and all. You know you have the wife's blessing," she added, softly. "If you can work your way around the demands of the job, I think the two of you have every chance of being happy together. Don't let a Victorian throwback like Howard Maddocks color your judgment, Chad. You and Doug are a couple; if I can see that, why can't you?"

"Because he scares the living shit out of me," he told her seriously. "He's so many people I don't know."

"And some of them love you, don't they?"

He did not answer immediately. He had turned his sightless gaze towards the window with its vista of green parkland, icing-sugar masonry, colorful planting and a sky of tranquil blue. He was asking himself that very same question and trying to find an honest answer. "I think so," he admitted at length.

Kirsten sat back in her seat. "Then hang on in there," she advised. "Maddocks can probably be won round eventually – he's just a dinosaur. He was never in favor of relaxing the rules on gays in the military in the first place and he likes you about as much as he likes me, and for very similar reasons. A strong gay man is an oxymoron as far as he's concerned."

"Like 'military intelligence'?"

"Just like. Women and gay guys are equal lowest in Howard's estimation, and he despises Doug for having anything to do with either one of us. It's up to you and me to prove him wrong, that's all. I don't know about you, Chad, but I get itchy shoulder-blades around the man."

"I know what you mean," Ryan told her, with a weary sigh. "We can cope with our enemies without difficulty, but may Heaven protect us from the machinations of our friends."

6.

Two weeks afterwards the First Lady flew to Nigeria to honor her volunteer commitment with MSF, and on the same day Berry and her agents set off for Florida to stay with Kirsten's parents. For a few days the routine continued much as before even in their absence, but then Kearney and Booth became involved in preparing for the first of a series of strategic meetings with European premiers, and Ryan took advantage of the opportunity to begin looking at apartments and houses in the city suitable for Presidential use. It was a dispiriting exercise, however, and he was glad to abandon it midway through the second week to fit in the promised visit to Berry and her grandparents.

Kirsten's parents were sprightly seniors with a house full of dogs and grandchildren and an open-hearted welcome for visitors of all shapes and sizes. This was something of a novelty in Ryan's existence and a source of extreme culture shock to him; family life had more or less passed him by, and he was almost overwhelmed by their eager inclusiveness even though he was to all intents and purposes merely a government employee. But Berry's Secret Service attendants were treated in exactly the same fashion and as they were young and energetic in a way Ryan could only envy, they seemed more than capable of keeping pace with their charge even at her most manic.

But Berry's grandparents were not so uncritically adoring that they could not relish the idea of getting the whole circus out of their elegantly graying hair for a few blissful hours, and so the prospect of 'Uncle Chad' pied-pipering their grand-daughter and her agents off to one of the local theme parks was greeted with enthusiasm by them both. Thus, suitably attired and with appropriate security, Ryan and Berry ate junk food and spent more time than he would have liked on white knuckle rides of various descriptions, and afterwards he stayed for dinner with the assembled family, shared a drink with Kirsten's father and heard his memories of service in Korea, and eventually returned to his hotel for the night. Shortly after lunch on the following day he was back at National, linking up with a White House pool car and driver for the short journey back to the building he was already beginning to think of as his home.

The President was in the informal sitting room tucked away at the end of its private corridor. He was lounging in jeans and a casual shirt, his hair mussed, his eyes tired, briefing papers spread out before him. However important his work might be, however, he abandoned it as soon as Ryan walked in and got up to hug him enthusiastically.

"Hey, welcome back. How was your flight? How's my daughter?" He ushered him to a chair and bustled about, shuffling files out of the way.

"She's great. So are her grandparents. They're wonderful people, aren't they?"

"The best." Kearney grinned and seated himself comfortably beside Chad. "Kirsten's pa tell you some of his war stories?"

"Certainly did. He's had a fascinating life."

"True. Did Berry make you go on that damn Death Ride thing?"

"Three times."

"Three?" The tone was frankly incredulous.

"She dared me, Doug; what did you expect me to do?"

"Call her bluff, I guess. Which of you went green first?"

"It was a close thing. But we were both able to eat dinner afterwards, so I guess there's no harm done."

"You're a brave man, Chad. Insane, but brave. Very brave."

And, since he knew they were not only talking about the Death Ride, Ryan merely nodded. "Thank you." But he found himself laughing. "Wouldn't you honestly think her life was exciting enough already?"

"Huh? Well, maybe she feels she can cope with just about anything when you're around. I know I do." Kearney had not really been concentrating on what he was saying. Now he set down his coffee cup and threw an amused look in Ryan's direction. "I look up and see you there and I know for certain everything's going to be okay. You have that effect on me, honey."

"You ... " Ryan began to speak, then stopped. "It's the same for me," he admitted, awkwardly.

"Yeah." The tone of Kearney's voice altered. "So, did you miss me?"

It was a revealing question; since the showdown with the Vice President Kearney had been in retreat, the shock of near-exposure driving him to discretion bordering on denial. Other than the occasional touch and a kiss or two snatched in the locker room or private sitting room, there had been no conduct to which Maddocks could have objected even if he had been present. Accepting the need for caution, however, was the easy part; reconciling abstinence with their desire for one another only demonstrated the magnitude of the gulf between logic and emotion and that this relationship conformed to the dictates of neither.

"Of course."

"You realize we promised discretion, rather than celibacy? We never said we'd stop wanting each other, just that we wouldn't do anything in public."

"No more misuse of Government facilities," smiled Ryan. "What exactly does that mean, anyway? No sex in the East Room during a reception?"

"Nor the Oval Office during a live broadcast," was the laughing reply.

"I'd probably do that, if you wanted."

"I know you would." The image was unreasonably distracting, however, and it was only with difficulty that Kearney fought his way back to practical and immediate considerations. He tapped the cover of the folder he had been examining before Ryan's arrival. "These are arrangements for the Prague summit – itineraries, meetings, the whole deal. It's going to be an absolute bitch. I hate traveling back east-west at night; you leave in the dark, you arrive in the dark, the sun's always hours behind you – I can never sleep."

"Maybe you'd prefer to go the long way home, across Russia and China. We don't have any enemies in either of those countries, do we?"

"Not as far as I can recall," the President smiled. "Anyway, I wish you were going with me. You'd love Prague, it's a beautiful city."

"And we'd spend our time strolling hand in hand and eating at sidewalk cafés, would we, just the two of us – not to mention the world's assembled media?"

"Doesn't sound the ideal vacation, does it? So, what will you be doing while I'm away?"

Ryan shrugged. "I figure it's the best chance to close up my apartment and move everything over, now that my room here's ready."

"I wish we could have found you something better," Kearney told him ruefully. "But it's only for a few months. Whatever happens in November everything's going to change anyway; either we'll find you better quarters, or we'll both be looking for somewhere else to live." He considered that prospect for a moment. "Not that it would be the worst thing in the world," he conceded. "Maybe I'd get more opportunities to have my wicked way with you. For the time being, it's not going to be easy finding occasions to be alone together. In fact," he concluded with deliberation, "this is the best chance we're going to have for a while."

Ryan blinked in astonishment. "This?"

"Here and now. I figure if we lock the door, close the drapes and play a loud movie, nobody ever needs to admit to knowing what we're up to." He stopped speaking, then resumed more quietly. "I don't know what else we can do, Chad; there's nowhere to go. I don't want to make out on the couch like a couple of horny teenagers any more than you do but the way you and I have been pussy-footing around one another lately, I'm about ready to drag you into a broom closet and I can't do that without the Secret Service getting nervous. This is probably the most we can hope for at the moment," he added, indicating the room, "if you think you can bear it?"

"I can if you can," was the quiet response. "I'll get the drapes."

"Good." Kearney got to his feet again and put his head out through the door. "Guys," he said, "no calls or interruptions for at least an hour. The Colonel and I are going to watch a movie."

And, if any member of the President's protection team wondered why it had suddenly become so urgently necessary for the Chief Executive and one of his more junior National Security Advisors to lock themselves in a darkened room on a sunny Saturday afternoon ostensibly for the purpose of watching a forty year old war movie, they were wise enough never to think of questioning it.

The night before the President's trip to Prague was the occasion for a white-tie dinner involving the leaders of the world's nuclear power industry. That evening, Ryan lingered in the private sitting room in the hope of snatching a last half-hour with Kearney before he left for his flight and drowsed in front of the television trying to absorb some film in which dinosaurs were taking over the Earth. It had been earnestly recommended as the kind of thing an exhausted President might enjoy watching to unwind but Ryan, who knew his President quite well by this stage, had become aware very early on that Kearney would find it more annoying than relaxing. For himself, he was long past the point where he could summon the energy to switch the wretched thing off. Instead he tucked his head against a cushion and let his eyes close, regardless of the death and destruction being wrought up there upon the TV screen.

Six days earlier, on this very couch, Ryan had been very thoroughly seduced; he had never imagined being so grateful for a movie epic's superfluity of explosions and machine-guns, not to mention diving planes and the sullen thud of heavy artillery. These had all conspired to make a suitable backdrop, somehow, for sweaty and almost-silent fumbling, for a rough avidity and an eventual shattering conclusion. They had ministered to one another with their hands perfectly effectively, but ultimately it had been soulless, functional, serving only a very limited purpose. Stripped of leisure and tenderness and the most basic dignity it had been an unsatisfactory encounter that, rather than assuaging the need that inspired it, had only emphasized the significance of their emotional connection. The inevitable conclusion was that it had not simply been sex that they were in want of after all, but somewhere along the way wrong choices had been made and the moment had been lost. Therefore he had decided to take advantage of this last brief window of opportunity in case Kearney should be in the mood for a lingering farewell; they were both beginning to learn, albeit the hard way, that their limited chances for being together should never be allowed to go to waste.

It was a little before 2 a.m. when the door to the small room opened and he heard Kearney's voice saying; "Chad?"

"Doug?" His eyes flew wide, and the next moment he was on his feet.

To his disappointment and confusion, however, Kearney was not alone; he and the Vice President, both in formal dinner suits, were accompanied by a general in dress uniform. Ryan struggled to stand to something resembling attention, disconcerted at being caught asleep wearing jeans and a tee-shirt and draped with unaccountable informality over a sofa in the President's private refuge. "Ummm, Mr President, Mr Vice President, I … "

"Relax," Kearney said, with a twist of his mouth. "I'm sorry we disturbed you. And this is not a 'Mr President' moment, this is a 'Doug' moment. Okay?"

"Yes." His whole body relaxing, Ryan grinned. "Okay."

"The guy's brought coffee." Kearney indicated a waiter who had followed them in. "We need to switch off the TV; there's something I want to talk to you about."

A moment later, Ryan had done what the hero had so far failed to do and killed off the dinosaurs; now he prepared to listen attentively to Doug instead.

Kearney waited until the waiter had left again and the door was closed behind him, and then his manner changed; his shoulders lost their rigidity as he took a long stride across to the silver tray. Without a word of explanation, the President began pouring coffee for everyone.

"Chad, you know General Barrington? George, this is Chad Ryan, the guy who saved my life a few months ago."

"Ryan. I think we've met, haven't we?"

"Sir." Amenities were kept to a minimum.

"Sit down, guys. George, show Chad the pictures you showed me."

Barrington was clutching a buff folder which he passed over without demur. The mutinous look on the Vice President's face seemed to indicate that he had not approved this course of action, but that for once he had ended up on the losing side of a battle of wills with the President.

"You remember that petrochemical plant in the Tien Shan mountains?" Kearney spoke to Ryan as he handed coffee to Maddocks and Barrington. "I know Mitch filled you in on some of the details; did he also happen to mention that we were hoping to have someone sample the contents of the trucks?"

"Yes sir, he did." Despite Kearney's request, it was impossible to mix business with pleasure; as long as he was being consulted in his professional capacity, Ryan was more comfortable making use of the title.

"Unfortunately," said Maddocks, harshly, "our guys have turned up dead."

"Which suggests that whatever's in those trucks the Chinese don't want us to examine it," Kearney completely grimly.

Ryan looked up at him. "Do we know how they died?"

"I'm afraid we do. They were crushed, probably under a load of stone. Their bodies were discovered two hundred and fifty miles away at a road construction site. The local authorities are calling it a tragic accident to two stray western tourists – after which of course they also accidentally mislaid the paperwork and cremated the bodies before anybody thought to tell us. We've got a witness who believes the men were killed at the freight yard and dumped where they were found a couple of days later. It's always easier transporting a body after it's dead."

Ryan nodded. "I'm sorry," he said.

"Yeah," acknowledged Kearney.

"The point, Colonel," put in Maddocks, "is that we're not anxious to commit more men to this operation until we have a better idea what's going on. We're not getting satellite pictures of train movements, indicating that they're being carefully timed, but we do have some pretty well-informed guesstimations of the amount of material already removed from the site."

"Enough for a tunnel all the way to Holofernes?" asked Ryan, unblinking.

"Three times over," the Vice President confirmed.

"Jesus, they've got Cheyenne Mountain down there."

"At the very least," said Barrington. "And fifteen hundred men."

"Enough for a whole town," Ryan mused. "Living quarters, medical facilities, processing, storage. They're going to need shielding, presumably lead and concrete; there must be massive amounts of materials going in."

"Also carefully timed," Maddocks told him. "And not from the

Kyrgyz side."

"No. That figures." Ryan looked up. "What is it you need from me, Mr President?"

Kearney's expression indicated approval of this businesslike approach. "I want you to work with the Vice President while I'm away," he said. "I won't discuss this on even the most secure circuit from Eastern Europe, so for the next couple of days you'll have to be my eyes and ears. Advise Howard exactly as you would advise me."

"Yes, sir."

"We'll talk again when I get back from Prague," Kearney concluded. "Howard, George, go on ahead will you? I need a moment with Chad."

Maddocks got to his feet and, trailed by the slow-moving Barrington, left the room. Kearney stood, too. He walked over and put the coffee cups back on the tray; despite years of cocooned luxury in houses full of servants he had never quite lost the courtesies of a less privileged past.

"How was your dinner?" Ryan asked, rising to move towards him.

"Boring as hell. I'll never know why I had to dress up like a penguin to get those guys to channel some of their profits into medical research. They're willing enough to create the problems, especially when it comes to occupational cancers, but not so enthusiastic about solving them; they seem to think there's an inexhaustible supply of fresh human beings waiting to be fed into their furnaces. And right at the point when I was finally getting rid of them and planning to spend a little time with you, George turned up with that report. It seemed like a good opportunity to get you and Howard working together for a change."

"I don't suppose he was very keen on the idea, was he?"

Kearney shook his head. "Don't make the mistake of underestimating him, Chad. He may not be much fun but the man's sharp enough politically and he recognizes ability when he sees it. Plus, he doesn't have to like you to respect you and work with you; after all, you don't like him!"

"True."

They were standing face to face now, and Kearney's hand took a possessive hold on Ryan's jeans-covered backside as Chad moved into his personal space, hands sliding smoothly over the front of the man's dress-shirt.

"Damn," said Kearney, "we're out of time." His lips came to rest softly in Ryan's blond hair. "I was hoping we might get an hour or so together, but I have to leave. I wasn't planning to travel in this outfit, I'll have to change on the plane. You want to ride out to Andrews with me in the car?"

"If you like." He managed to make his acceptance sound almost casual whereas in fact his heart was racing wildly at even having been asked.

"Thanks." A moment of silence, in which Kearney's arms closed around him more tightly. "Chad, you're there when I need you and you're whatever I need you to be. It seems to me all I do in this relationship is take. There must be something I can do in exchange. What can I do to make you happy?"

"You can stand here like this and ask me that?" Astonished, Ryan drew back and looked up into his face. "Don't you know I constantly wonder what I ever did to deserve anything from you at all? You don't owe me a thing, Doug. Being with you is enough."

Not convinced, Kearney bit his lip. "No, there has to be something. Ask me. Let me start giving something back."

"Anything?"

"Anything."

A distant expression crossed Ryan's face. "There is one thing I'd like," he conceded, smiling.

"Uh-huh?"

Ryan took a deep breath. "I'd like us to spend a night together some time. I just want to wake up next to you one morning and pretend you're really mine."

"That's all?" Kearney was incredulous. "No car, no condo, no polo ponies?"

Ryan laughed, delightedly burying his face in the President's shirt-front as though falling into some childhood snow-bank. "Where would I keep polo ponies?" he asked. "I'm supposed to be moving into the White House; there wouldn't be room. And all I've ever wanted was your time."

"Which is exactly what I can't give you at the moment."

"I know that. I'll survive."

"Although waking up with you is definitely on the agenda – and so are nights together, as soon and as often as we get the chance. Which may not be often," he conceded.

"That's okay," Ryan told him. "I'm sure you'll be worth waiting for."

"Glad to hear it, Colonel Ryan," the President told him, closing in for a deeply indulgent and very thorough kiss. "Because I'm pretty sure you will be, too."

Thirty-five minutes later, with the President still dressed in his dinner suit – although he now carried the tailcoat over his arm – the two men plunged side by side into the rear of a limousine waiting under the Portico.

"I'll be home late Wednesday," Kearney told him, brusquely. "Stay in touch with Berry while I'm away, will you?"

"I will. We've already fixed it up."

"Good." Kearney's face twisted into an ironic grin. "Sometimes I think you're a better father than I am, Chad."

Ryan's reaction was one of astonishment. "That's completely bizarre."

"I know. But you can be there for my daughter in ways that I can't. I wish you'd change your mind about having Secret Service protection of your own, though." It was an old debate, much rehearsed between them, which had remained unresolved and looked likely to do so again.

"I wouldn't be comfortable," Ryan told him. "I can't imagine how I'd feel if someone was hurt trying to protect me. And anyway, you know the Vice President would call it 'egregious misapplication of finite Government resources'. "

"He probably would, at that. But we're coming to the point where I may have to pull rank on you. I don't like the thought of you not having your own agent."

Reluctantly Ryan acknowledged that he had been on the losing end of this battle ever since the subject was first raised. "Do you have someone in mind?"

"I do. Olivia Hernandez. She's one of Joel's best people and she knows about ... well – she knows, okay?"

"Why does she want to transfer off the First Lady's team?"

"She doesn't but she's due for rotation, and she's asked to be assigned to you. I think you'd work well together. Kick it around while I'm away, will you?"

"All right, I promise. But it'll feel strange."

"This whole deal feels strange, if you ask me. I still look at myself in the mirror every morning and ask why any rational electorate would want me as their President; everything else is so surreal that I stopped believing in it years ago."

"Does that include me?"

"Yeah, you, me, everything." Kearney looked out towards the sleeping city. "I need a vacation. I've been trying to get to my house in Vermont for months but I couldn't find a decent excuse. You'd go with me, wouldn't you? I want to show you the place."

"Of course. But I don't see how." The long lenses of the paparazzi would be no more appealing for the change of venue, and the kind of vacation Kearney had in mind would warrant a dramatic increase in media interest. Was there nowhere on the planet a hard-working President could find a little peace and quiet?

"We'll think of something," Kearney assured him, with a grimace, folding Ryan's hand into his own as the silent streets swept past their windows.

They were waved through the perimeter at Andrews Air Force Base by gray-faced and expressionless men, rigidly formal as they passed; the outriders peeled off and their driver took a wide, sinuous course like the turning circle of an ocean liner, bringing the motorcade into formation under the shadow of the wing of Air Force One. Despite it being scarcely 3 a.m., there was a group of people waiting at the foot of the steps to the Presidential 747, including the National Security Advisor who had absented himself from the nuclear industry dinner more than an hour previously and found the opportunity to change out of his evening clothes in the interim.

Kearney and Ryan piled out of the car and stood for a moment looking at the shining blue and white bulk of the aircraft. Then Kearney stepped away, conscious of the party at the foot of the boarding stairs. After two or three strides, however, a thought seemed to strike him and he turned back, a tall figure in a dinner suit with a crumpled tailcoat over one arm, to grip the shoulder of the jeaned and tee-shirted nonentity waiting beside the car.

Ryan looked into his eyes and saw there the affection usually kept strictly in reserve. Although he did not doubt the discretion of everyone present, this was a more public location than they would normally have chosen for such an intimate scene and he was suddenly afraid that the President intended to kiss him in front of everyone.

"Doug … " he warned.

"I know. I'm going. Be here when I get back."

"Always. I love you."

Ryan had not known he was going to say it; had not even known he was thinking it, but somehow the words were out before he was ready. And then again, why should he not say it? Was it really a secret between them, after all?

Although there was no possibility of their words being overheard, Kearney was careful to make no verbal reply. Instead the grin on his face spread from ear to ear and for a moment he looked far, far younger than his years.

"You know, we're going to have to do something about that," he smiled. "When I get back." Then, with a spring in his stride, he turned away again. Ryan watched as he greeted those who were waiting for him, slapped Booth on the shoulder and bounded up the steps to the plane as though relishing the trip ahead. He made not the slightest attempt to look behind him.

Ryan stuffed his hands into his jeans pockets and waited, fair hair blowing in the breeze, while Air Force One taxied and took off into the night. Only when its tail-lights had vanished from view did he turn back to the limo and, with a nod to the driver, quietly ask to be taken back to the shelter and safety of the White House.

Over the weekend, Ryan was fully occupied with packing and preparing to return his apartment to the possession of his landlord. He had not acquired many belongings in the course of a peripatetic service life and these were quickly dealt with, but he had resolved to make a ruthless sweep through his civilian wardrobe and dispose of things he could not imagine himself ever wearing in the remodeled version of his life. There were also neighbors, briefly known, amongst whom he would be distributing his few surviving plants. He had even been invited to a farewell dinner and although he enjoyed it he had found it difficult not to give details of where he would be living in future and why he was making the change. In a government town like DC, however, most people knew better than to ask too many questions; Ryan's refusal to discuss his plans received knowing responses and the subject changed. He would be permitted to take his secrets with him when he left, and the memory of his acquaintance would probably only endure as long as the last of his orphaned house-plants stayed alive.

One more late evening and one long morning were all he needed to see the job completed; if everything went according to plan he would be installed in his small but efficient staff bedroom in the White House Residence long before Kearney and his entourage embarked on their return journey from Prague.

That evening, dusk had already fallen as he bustled up the steps at the Dupont Circle subway, his mind several thousand miles away, musing on the day's television pictures of Kearney sitting in the kind of palatially-splendid room nobody ever used except to take photographs in, his solid frame perched on a delicate antique chair, apparently in serious dialogue with a corpulent baby-faced individual with all the charm of a nuclear winter. It would have taken someone who knew Doug really well to detect that he was even slightly ill at ease; that little gesture of fiddling with his shirt-cuff and the thumbnail dragging thoughtfully across the lower lip were indicators that the man hated every minute of what he was doing and could not wait to be at home – or, at the very least, anywhere but where he was. And Ryan was missing him, too; it was astonishing how quickly he'd become used to having the warmth of Kearney to cling to, even if only briefly, and those deeply affectionate tones whispering reassurances close to his ear.

He was, in short, so preoccupied with scenes far removed from those around him that he did not have either the time or the energy to spare for incidental matters like personal safety, and thus he was not as conscious of his surroundings as he should have been. It was no surprise, therefore, that he ran headlong into the compact body of a man hurrying at speed down the same steps, but as he opened his mouth to apologize Ryan heard the word "Wallet!" and was slammed against the wall while urgent and determined hands set to work rummaging through his clothing.

"No!"

It was a stupid, nonsensical thing to say; as if shouting could prevent this! Belatedly Ryan's brain began to work and he attempted to resist, but the man had a considerable height and weight advantage over him and seemed to be in the throes of desperation. In jagged flashes like the flickers of an eccentric strobe he tried to fight, grabbing his attacker's wrist only to have an elbow land sharply in his stomach and a fist pummel viciously into his face. He staggered, his feet went from under him, and suddenly he was being kicked over and over again and his head was in contact with a wall or a floor or a step, and although he did not lose consciousness he was unable to hear because his head was full of sound and pain and he coughed away blood that filled his mouth. That was when he understood that he was nothing without Douglas Kearney; that if only Doug had been there he would have torn this bastard's head from his shoulders and played football with it, but that on his own Chad Ryan could do little but lean back bleeding against a tiled wall while someone he didn't know helped himself to his watch and wallet and cell phone and was gone before he could find a coherent word of protest in response.

And then an Asian woman, a tourist, was comforting him, and he recognized the blue lights of a paramedic ambulance, and he managed to say; "Call the White House" just before he passed out.

Over the next several hours Ryan was in and out of consciousness, drifting between light and pain and peripherally aware of things that made no sense whatsoever and only linked into a rational narrative when the mechanism to process thought had once again become available to him. Someone addressing him as "Mr Ryan" advised him that a call had been made; a person would be coming from the White House as soon as humanly possible. Then a hand slipped into his and a voice he thought he knew from somewhere told him everything would be fine, and he said "Doug," but the hand was slim and cool and feminine and the fingers on his brow had an almost impersonal touch, and even in his semi-conscious condition he felt cheated. Whoever was sitting beside him, loyally attempting to bring him comfort, it was obviously not the man he loved.

But then again it could not be. Kearney was too important and too far away and they had both had far too many frozen stares from the Vice President to risk being seen together outside the White House. It was some other sweet soul who was here in Doug's place, and however grateful he might have been for her generosity and concern, he wanted Doug. Reduced to his core components by a casual crime, he knew only that his heart ached for Kearney, that he was not and could not be beside him, and that whatever they had shared so far it was never going to amount to anything like enough.

7.

"They thought you were crazy," Hernandez said, softly. Somehow it was morning and light was flooding into the room; a room filled with flowers; a room that was not in any hospital. "'Call the White House, call the White House.' The First Lady wanted to turn right around and get on the next flight home as soon as she knew. The President talked her out of it, but he couldn't do a thing about his daughter; she's on her way."

"Berry?" He tried the name, brutally conscious of a stitch holding the corner of his mouth.

"You know how she feels about you. She probably wants to give you twenty four hour nursing care and I don't know how her father is going to take that."

The fog was slow to clear. Something about white tiles and pain and blood was lodged in Ryan's mind, along with the impressive grip of fingers that had crushed his almost to the bone.

"Was he here?" he asked, almost afraid to hear the answer.

"Was he here?" Hernandez repeated with a rueful smile. "The President? Yes, he was here. He flew home a day early. He'll be back, too, as soon as he gets through his meeting with the Attorney General. A couple of hours. Maybe you can manage to be awake this time? Last time he came up, you were fast asleep."

Not knowing whether to believe her words or not, Ryan decided he was too exhausted to be chagrined.

"Is this his room?"

"Yes."

Propped on a mountain of pillows, he looked around to the best of his ability; there were directions in which his head refused to turn, aching muscles preventing some movements. It did not take long to decide that if he had to sleep every night in this room it would drive him insane with its sombre decor and furnishings. No wonder he had never been invited to share Kearney's bed; even the most passionate of lusts would have wilted in this oppressive setting.

"I wish you could have seen him," Hernandez enthused. "He came straight to the hospital from Andrews the moment Air Force One touched down. All our people said was that someone from the President's staff would be coming but they didn't say who. Freaked them out when they realized they had the President himself – and in a pissy frame of mind, too. Apparently the Czech premier filled him up with vodka before he got on the plane, and he'd had a ten hour flight with hardly any sleep. After that, you can imagine he was in no mood for them all panicking about security."

"Oh God." Part of Ryan's consciousness was embarrassed at being the cause of such pandemonium, but deep down there was an unholy thrill at the notion of Kearney reducing a hospital to rubble for his sake. He had only to close his eyes to imagine the expression on the President's face, the intensity of his focus as he snapped out orders and questions and dealt scathingly with expressions of astonishment.

"He told them he was your next of kin," Hernandez went on, knowing she was feeding some atavistic need.

"He was right." Tired and disoriented as he was, he could not keep possessive pride out of his tone. "There's no-one else."

"He didn't look like a President. I think they had him in ground crew fatigues from Andrews or something. He came in surrounded by agents and the doctors didn't recognize him at first. Then they started freaking out because they hadn't had cleaners through in the last half-hour. Do you know what he told them?"

"That it made a nice change to be somewhere that hadn't just been repainted in his honor?"

"Pretty much. He said 'How soon can I take him home?', and they said … "

"'The sooner the better, and let us get on with our work'?"

"Right. And the next thing anybody knows he's carrying you out to the car and dragging me along with him, and three of our guys got left behind and had to come over in a cab."

"He … ?"

"Yeah," she said, her tone softening. "He carried you. Picked you up as if you weighed no more than Berry, and put you in the limo all by himself – and nobody dared try telling him he couldn't. All the way home he's giving me orders not to leave you unless he says so, and when we got here … You don't argue with a President in that frame of mind, believe me."

"Which is why I ended up in his bed?"

"One of the reasons, sure. He called the First Lady and told her all about it, and after that he sat down and held your hand so long I thought he was going to fall asleep, so I put a blanket round him and he looked at me … " She stopped abruptly. "Chad, if I thought somebody felt that way about me I swear I'd die happy. If you didn't know it before, I have to tell you – that man loves you a lot."

He closed his eyes, absorbing her words as though they were rays of sunlight. "If he does," he said distantly, "he hasn't said so."

"No? Well, maybe he hasn't figured it out for himself yet," she mused. "Isn't that just like a man?"

"Yes, it is." He fell silent for a while, his eyes remaining closed, as he thought about Kearney tearing up the hospital and stealing him away into the night. Part of him wished he had at least been conscious enough to burrow his head into Kearney's chest and listen to his heart, and feel the strength of the man enfold him in its protective embrace. It was the most open demonstration he had received yet of the President's feelings – and he had missed it all! "So you'll be with me from now on, Olivia?"

"I will," Hernandez told him. "As long as the President wants me to."

"And you were at the hospital." The slender feminine fingers wrapped around his own had undoubtedly been hers.

"Almost before your head touched the pillow," she confirmed. "You were asking everybody to call the White House, and eventually somebody decided to take it seriously. Luckily, whoever was on the switchboard recognized your description because you didn't have any ID by that stage and you were in no state to answer questions. So they passed it up the line and all hell broke loose. You know who called me? The Vice President. 'Get right over there and hold his hand', he said. So I did."

"The Vice President?"

"Yes sir. He did exactly what the President would want him to do – made sure you were safe, then started making plans to bring you back here. 'Course I don't think he planned for you to end up in the President's bed," she added cheekily.

"Now or at any other time."

"No, that's true," conceded Olivia. "Just so long as you realize it's pretty much okay with the rest of us."

Ryan was still drowsing some hours later when the door opened and closed quietly and his hand was taken in a warm, strong grip. He opened his eyes and for the longest time reveled in the sight of Kearney leaning over him, enfolding Ryan's hand in his, a strange lop-sided half-smile hovering on his face as if he were secretly torn between delight and embarrassment.

"So you're back with us at last." Kearney sat down on the bed. "How're you feeling?"

"I think I must be dead," was the brief response. "Everything hurts." Ryan struggled to sit up, but a hand on the shoulder stopped him.

"Stay where you are. You're not too badly damaged – just sprains and mild concussion, apart from the broken wrist."

Ryan grimaced. "Apparently I'm going to have spectacular bruises. Are these flowers all from you?" he added, indicating sprays and baskets around the room, each stuffed with colorful blooms. The scent was almost overpowering on such a warm day.

"No. Just most of them. Kirsten's parents sent some, Mitch and Jeannie, Angela on behalf of Kirsten ... I think there's even a bouquet from the Secret Service; it probably has a card saying 'I told you so!'"

At this point, inspiration seemed to desert Kearney; clearly he was uncomfortable making small-talk with the sick. Ryan recollected the President apologizing for not visiting him in the hospital and wondered whether fear of illness or infirmity had been the reason rather than a crowded schedule; it was rare to see Douglas Kearney not fully in command of any situation.

"Berry's home," he offered awkwardly. "She rushed back as soon as she heard the news. She won't believe you're alive until she's examined you yourself. Do you feel up to seeing her yet?"

"Not right now. I'd rather just have you. I missed you."

"I know." Kearney hung his head. "I should have taken you with me."

"Oh, sure," Ryan told him, with a gently mocking laugh. "That would have played well. 'Your Excellency, this is my boyfriend. I brought him along because my Vice President won't let me sleep with him in the White House'. Great way to start an international incident."

"You underestimate the guy," Kearney chuckled. "I'm sure he'd have taken one look and wanted you for himself. Or he'd have filled you up with vodka and tried to make a fool of you like he did me. Do me a favor; if I ever look like I'm going to drink that stuff again, stop me. They gave me a dozen cases to bring home; we should have poured it into the tanks instead of shipping it in the hold. I'm going to have to wrap it up as Christmas presents or serve it at a reception for someone we don't much care about, just to get rid of it all."

"Give it to the British," Ryan suggested. "They don't know good booze from bad."

"Good idea." Kearney's unease had begun to evaporate and he had taken Ryan's hand again, this time as though it was the most natural gesture in the world. "Why didn't I think of that?"

"And how was business?" asked Ryan, smiling.

Kearney grimaced. "Business was good. We built bridges. Business I can do, Chad. It's the parties afterwards I have trouble with. You'd be amazed how many people seem to think it's a good idea to throw booze and girls at me; half the time I don't know whether they're being hospitable or looking for something to blackmail me with."

"Good job I wasn't there. I might have seriously cramped your style."

"If you were there, Chad, you couldn't have been mugged at Dupont Circle. I'm told your watch and cell phone will have been sold on by now and your wallet's probably somewhere in the Potomac. I'm sorry it happened."

"No need to apologize; it wasn't your fault – and even if you'd been with me you couldn't have done anything except get yourself hurt too."

"You're wrong, it is my fault. It's my fault because I'm supposed to be running things and I can't stop this happening to the people I care about. And the guy who robbed you is also a victim; the country failed him. I failed him. I failed you, after everything you did for me. I don't know where I'd have been these last few weeks if you hadn't been here to hold my hand."

"That doesn't make you responsible for everything that happens to me," Ryan reminded him. "I'm an adult with free will. I could have taken a cab or a pool car, but I didn't. I wasn't targeted for being the President's boyfriend, Doug; there was nothing personal about it. The guy just reacted instinctively when I bumped into him; he probably wasn't even thinking about robbing anybody before that. Give yourself a break; you're Douglas Kearney, not … not Captain America."

"Captain America? How can I be Captain America? How can I make the world safe for democracy when I can't even make one city safe for my own … " He stopped, the next word so far beyond him that it seemed unlikely he would ever reach it. He tried again. "My … "

"Your cute, plucky sidekick?" Ryan was well aware of the word Kearney had choked on.

"My cute, plucky sidekick," Kearney repeated gratefully. "That would make you … Bucky Barnes, I guess."

"What a memory you have, Cap." Squeezing the hand he held, Ryan looked into an expression that was a compound of confusion and annoyance and frustration. "So, what's on your agenda this morning, Mr President? Is there anything happening in the world I should know about?"

"A political assassination in Bolivia, and a school roof in Texas has collapsed on top of eight people. Oh, and the State of Michigan is taking legal action to try to evict a pair of beavers from their dam; I'm going to have to give them a little friendly advice."

"The State of Michigan? Or the beavers?"

"Michigan. The beavers are doing fine without my help." A tentative smile had taken the place of the worried expression. "In the short term, I'm going back to clear my desk; that'll take the rest of the day. As soon as it's finished this President is going to develop laryngitis and cancel his engagements for the weekend. We're going to Vermont tomorrow, the two of us. I've been on the phone all morning arranging it."

"Two of us?" An incredulous repetition.

"Plus Berry – there'll be no leaving her behind, so I'm going to have to tell her all about you and me. Kirsten's already started preparing the ground, but my daughter's not stupid; she'll have guessed by now how it is between us."

"She will?"

"Kids are smarter than you'd think," Kearney told him. "And Berry's been raised not to see gender as a barrier to a loving relationship; we wanted her to understand any choice she made would be fine with us, and you can't start too early explaining that sort of thing. Anyway, we're also going to have the Secret Service and the guy with the 'football' – you know, the briefcase with all the nuclear codes in it – and if they haven't guessed already they're soon going to work it out. This is what you asked me for before I went away – somewhere we can wake up together and forget the world for a while. You and I need a little time to ourselves, Chad; this is the best I can offer."

"It sounds wonderful," Ryan admitted, reckoning he had made Kearney suffer long enough and vaguely amazed at the intensity with which the President had tried to sell him the idea. Didn't the man realize by now that all he needed to do was snap his fingers?

"It will be," Kearney assured him. "I intend to make sure of it personally."

"In that case," was the delighted response, "how can I possibly refuse?"

Chad Ryan slept that night in the President's bed, but the President did not. Kearney also managed to keep Berry away from him that evening but she was there at breakfast, although obviously on her very best behavior; her eyes were as large as saucers.

"Wow," she said, impressed. "You're purple."

"Thank you."

Ryan's bruised eye-socket was, in fact, three distinct colors – blue-gray, purple, and a kind of dull yellow – and the side of his face was distended like that of a man with acute toothache. His right wrist was in a cast and he had been provided with a black silk arm sling, which he felt made him look as if he were milking his injuries for all he was worth. He would sooner have done without it but the President, predictably, would hear of no such thing.

Ryan and Berry stared at one another over the table as a steward poured tea. He did not mention the elephant in the room between them, and she seemed supremely oblivious of it.

"Where's your father?" he asked instead. Kearney was nowhere to be seen.

Berry shrugged. "With the Vice President and Uncle Mitch, I think. We're not going in the 747 today," she added enthusiastically.

"We're not?" He wasn't sure why he had imagined they were, now that he came to think about it, except that he'd supposed that Air Force One would still be on the tarmac at Andrews and probably easy to turn around for another flight.

"No, we're going in the Gulfstream, the one that usually flies 'Tailgate'."

He blinked, trying to pin down the name. All of a sudden it came to him; 'Tailgate' was the codename of the executive jet that accompanied Air Force One like a pilot fish accompanying a shark, bringing backup equipment and additional personnel. Being smaller and more maneuverable, it often took the President's advance team ahead of the main convoy or carried the First Lady to rendezvous with her husband when they had been on separate engagements.

"We did it this way before," said Berry. "On the campaign, we had a Gulfstream and flew into Burlington. My dad says the runway isn't long enough for a 747; you need at least 10,000 feet and it's only 8,000."

"Really?" In all his years in the Air Force, these were things Chad hadn't ever needed to know. He had never been a pilot, never logged as much as a single hour on a simulator, only ever flown as a passenger.

"They'll send cars to take us to Great Aunt Martha's house. That's what we call it but she didn't live there. She was in the Silver Threads Nursing Home until she died. She thought I was my grandmother. She called me Berenice."

"Well, that is your name," Ryan reminded her, in confusion. Truth to tell, he was struggling; the attempt to hold a knife in his left hand was not going particularly well and there was marmalade on his plaster cast.

"Duh," said Berry. "You're 'Charles' but everybody calls you 'Chad'. Suppose somebody started calling you 'Charlie' and thinking you were your grandpa? How would you like that?"

He stopped and thought about it, and decided she was right. "Actually," he admitted, "I don't think I'd like it very much at all."

"You see," said Berry, triumphantly, and he was aware that she thought she had won the point – and that she was probably right – but he wasn't sure exactly what the point had been.

Three hours later, the Gulfstream was turning eastwards over the sparkling water of Lake Champlain, making a last lazy loop preparatory to lining up with the main runway at BTV. Kearney, Berry and Ryan were attended by Olivia Hernandez and three other Secret Service agents, plus the guy with the nuclear football and two of his alternates. They also had a couple of domestic staff in tow, and someone sent along by the President's personal physician simply to keep an eye on Ryan's developing bruises. Berry had taken pity on this individual and was even now sitting beside him delivering what appeared to be a University-level tutorial on some subject of abiding teenage interest, and the poor man's eyeballs were slowly beginning to counter-rotate.

As they came to a halt on the tarmac, half a dozen airport emergency vehicles ripped loose from their stations and surrounded the plane. A couple of armored Cherokees swooped into place within their cordon and a little to one side was a bus for staff and luggage. In between, however, was a small honor guard of officers with gleaming medals and expectant expressions. Kearney looked at them in mild annoyance.

"Damn protocol," he growled. "You tell them it's an informal thing and you want to keep it under the radar and they send thirty guys and a marching band."

Ryan glanced out apprehensively. Four uniformed men were lined up on the tarmac, with the same number of armed sentries standing a little further off trying to look unimpressed.

"Just for once," Kearney continued, "I'd like it to be one guy and a dog. I'd even carry my own bag."

"It's a matter of respect for the office," Ryan protested weakly.

"I know. But I need to get away from the Presidency for a while. I wish they'd get the message."

The door of the plane was flung open. The football colonel had stepped down and was standing to one side, with Olivia Hernandez next to him. Another of the agents was supervising the unloading of a small quantity of luggage.

"Maybe they will, this weekend," was the tired reply. The painkillers had been cutting in and out all morning and Ryan was due another dose. The nagging ache in his wrist and the bruises elsewhere on his body seemed to be sapping his energy and he could no longer be angelically tolerant of Kearney's discomfort.

Kearney accepted the reproof in good humor. "Okay, Bucky, let's get you out of here and introduce you to some people. Just relax and be your usual sweet self, and remember these guys are on our side."

"Yes, Mr President," Ryan told him, gratefully allowing himself to be helped up out of his seat.

The formal introductions did not take long. Ryan was addressed as 'Colonel' by the officers, all of whom held the same rank or higher, and not for the first time he was aware of how seriously skewed his universe had become since meeting the President. Now, people for whom he would previously have had to stand at attention and to whom he should have been deferring were treating him with almost the same level of respect as the man who stood beside him.

"Try not to go to sleep in the car," Kearney warned him softly as they stepped away from the reception party. "It's not much more than an hour from here." He gave one more quasi-formal wave, then ushered Ryan, Berry and Hernandez into the vehicle. "What did we tell them about rooms?" he asked the agent as the doors were closed and they began to move away easily.

Olivia glanced briefly at Berry. "To make up as many as they liked but not to expect them all to be slept in," she replied.

"They understood?"

"Yes, sir. They understood."

"Good." He turned back to Ryan. "My house is a mess," he explained. "It needs five years of solid work before it's habitable again. But back during the campaign, I took a lease on another place in the same valley. The staff there are all people I've known for years. It's about as private as we're ever going to get, considering all the security and communications personnel I have to travel with. And there's plenty to do if you get bored with my company. You can swim, ride, shoot – there are movies, a library … "

"Doug, you don't have to try so hard," Ryan protested. "Have I ever been bored with your company yet?"

"No. But then we've never spent much more than three or four hours together. And I'll have work to do, unfortunately, but I'm sure you and Berry can keep each other entertained while I'm busy."

"Okay." He glanced at the girl, who was grinning back at him. There was no doubting that she and her father had had the intended conversation, and that she was in favor of whatever sleeping arrangements might have been proposed. "I don't know whether I should be trying to swim just yet, but I could probably ride if somebody helped me up on the horse. Movies sound good too."

"I wasn't thinking of horses," Kearney supplied, with a wicked grin. "That's more Berry's territory than mine." For a moment it almost seemed as if an off-color remark might spill out of his mouth, and Ryan and Olivia glanced sharply at one another in anxiety. Then the President said, wistfully, "Actually, I've got a motorcycle here and I don't get many chances to ride it. If you can hold on with your good arm, I'll take you for a tour of the estate."

"I can hold on," Ryan assured him. "I'll tie myself to the bike if I have to. Thank you, I'd love to do that."

"You're welcome. Give yourself a chance to settle in and recover from the journey and maybe we'll do that this afternoon. Just give me time to change my clothes and start to feel like the kind of no-account loser who spends his weekends dirt-biking."

"You mean the kind who'll never amount to anything in this world?"

"Yeah, that kind," agreed the President with a grin.

An hour and a half later, their modest motorcade rolled up over a stone driveway and halted in front of an elegant colonial clapboard house painted a non-traditional barn red. Its door and window frames and its shutters were picked out in glossy white, and it sat confidently in its landscape daring anyone to criticize its choice of attire. Mature trees and gardens surrounded it, and a paddock containing three horses occupied the foreground. Almost before they had stopped moving, Berry was out of the car and holding a conversation with the animals; Kearney and Ryan, however, took their time, stepping into the sunny afternoon and drawing appreciative breaths of cool fresh air.

"You're gonna love this place," Kearney promised. "This is the Ford House. It used to be owned by my mother's family; in fact she was born here. Unfortunately it had to be sold sixty years ago when my grandfather died." He paused. "Wait till you see the decor; it was fashionable once."

A White House steward was waiting for them in the doorway; their luggage was already being unloaded from the bus.

"Relax," said Kearney. "All the staff here are blind and deaf – metaphorically, anyway." They stepped inside. "Sitting room, dining room, library." Through the open doorways it was possible to see heavy brocade curtains, gleaming furniture, old books, and a frantic wallpaper design of red and green cabbages. "Communications post in the sun room at the back, handy for the kitchen and downstairs bathroom. Staff wing sleeps nine, and in the house itself we can take eight; this time it's you, me, Berry, the guys with the football and Dr Frankenstein."

"Franklyn."

"You say 'potato'," was the careless reply.

"Dr Potato," amended Ryan.

"You got it. Since I'll be working in the library that's pretty much off limits, but the rest of the place is up for grabs. Berry can show you around."

"Actually," said Ryan, "if you don't mind, I think I'd prefer to take some painkillers and try to sleep for an hour or two."

"Of course I don't mind." They had paused at the bottom of the stairs. "Gregor here will take care of you. The Blue Bedroom, Gregor?"

"Yes, sir."

"Okay then. Rest. We'll talk later." And without a further word Kearney handed Chad off to the steward and strode away to the communications post to re-establish contact with the world as it existed beyond the confines of the Green Mountain State.

It was a full two hours before Ryan resurfaced, and then he crawled downstairs and followed Berry's voice to the kitchen where she was keeping the Secret Service entertained. As the only child in a household of adults – serious-minded, purposeful adults at that – she was exploiting her captive audience to the full, and had browbeaten Hernandez and one of the colonels into playing a board game the rules of which seemed to be remarkably fluid. Olivia looked up in relief as he entered.

"Chad! Rescue me!"

He shook his head. "Not on your life." Then, more quietly, "Where's Doug?"

"In the barn." She stood up and pointed from the window. "That's where he keeps his motorcycle. He's probably polishing it or something; the First Lady swears he's passionately in love with the thing."

He looked away, flushing slightly. One of the local detachment of Secret Service guys, the ones who had set up security at the Ford House and maintained it in the absence of the First Family, was standing at the entrance to the barn smoking a cigarette. Since he could hardly have done this without Presidential imprimatur, it was a fair assumption that the man had been standing too close and probably testing his Chief Executive's otherwise formidable patience. That was not a situation on which Chad was particularly anxious to intrude.

"Are you going over?" Olivia was watching him in fascination.

"I don't think so. I wouldn't want to crowd him. I think I'll sit on the terrace and watch the sky a while."

"Sounds like a plan. You should never get between a guy and the love of his life, you know."

"Wouldn't dream of it," was the calm reply, and he wandered out to stretch himself on a steamer chair and take advantage of the shelter and the sun.

Later, as the three of them were settling down to dine on the terrace, Kirsten called from Lagos to talk to her daughter.

"It's nearly midnight there," Berry reported, returning to the table after the call. "She's going to sleep now and leave in the morning. She'll be at the White House late tomorrow our time; she says it's an eleven hour flight with a five hour time difference. Chad, you shouldn't be drinking that!"

Kearney had taken two bottles of beer out of the mini-fridge behind the rustic structure that passed for a bar counter and handed one over to Ryan.

"It's okay, sweetheart, he's taking ibuprofen; there's no reason not to drink."

"As long as I don't have to operate heavy machinery." Ryan accepted the bottle, smiling up at him.

"Well, you won't be driving the combine this evening." Kearney knocked the top off his beer and swallowed gratefully. "What else'd she say, honey?"

"That this stuff's private," said Berry. "About you and Chad. But I knew that anyway. Mom said we couldn't discuss it on the phone." She stopped and looked at them. "You do know it's no big deal, though, don't you?"

Ryan was regarding her thoughtfully. "Actually, it's a big deal for us," he pointed out.

"Well, yeah," was the easy response. "What I mean is, it's no big deal for me. In fact, I think it's great." There was a silence, then Berry continued. "You know my friend Jessica? Her father's doing the nanny and he doesn't care who knows it. And Aubretia's father made two of his assistants pregnant, one right after the other, and they both had little girls. And last year Casey's mom went off to Thailand with a guy she met at a rock festival and nobody knows where she is now. None of my friends' dads has ever had a boyfriend. It's really, really cool."

"Cool?" Her father almost choked on the word. "I never thought of it like that." He leaned toward her. "I'm glad you approve," he said.

"You understand you can't tell anybody, though, don't you?"

"Yeah, I do. But it can still be my secret weapon. Whenever Jessica's whining or Aubretia's showing off, I'll think about how lame it must be to have a father who only likes girls. A gay dad's just so much more interesting."

Ryan coughed awkwardly. "Sweetheart," he said, "you're the President's daughter; you shouldn't have to care about anybody else showing off."

"Aubretia has her own maid," was the devastating response. Then; "She's fifty and ugly so Aubretia's dad won't do the same to her. Aubretia says he can't keep it in his pants. I'm so glad you guys aren't anything like him."

8.

Half way through the meal, the first streaks of pink and lavender began to appear above them and later, as the evening disintegrated into good-humored chaos with everybody sampling everybody else's dessert, the sky split apart into layers of purple, orange, gray and silver. When it became too cold to sit outside, they retreated indoors to a sitting room furnished in countrified good taste, and piled onto the couch together to watch a forgettably silly movie. After it was over and the time came for Berry to go to bed, she retreated in good order, kissing both her father and his friend and leaving them relaxed, sleepy and alone.

"She's fantastic." Ryan was contemplating the way the light played through a globe of brandy Kearney had pushed into his hands. "Insane, but adorable, like the rest of you. She seems so calm about the whole business."

"She's shock-proof. And crazy about you – also like the rest of us." Kearney's arm snaked around his shoulders again, drew him in. "In the morning I'll show you the drawings for the other house. They're kind of grandiose – stables, sauna, big dining room, pool. But we don't have to do it all at once."

"A pool?"

"Sure. I'm going to need somewhere to seduce you, aren't I?"

"Of course." Despite himself, Ryan yawned. It had been a long day, and the sweet country air had filled his lungs so thoroughly that he had relaxed beyond anything he ever thought possible. He nestled against Kearney, feeling his bones turn to water. For a wonderful all-encompassing moment, he flowed around him and drew him in and there was no separateness between them – no separateness, and no intrusion of reality. He had never felt so securely welded to another person in his life before. Then there was a gentle sound against his ear and although his senses were almost completely distorted, Ryan heard and understood not only the words that were said but also those that were not.

"C'mon, honey," whispered the President. "I think it's time you and I were in bed."

They stepped together into their darkened room. The bed, antique oak piled with pillows, lay in a veil of moonlight; flimsy drapes stirred in a fickle breeze.

"It's strange," said Ryan, quietly, "not having to hide. I've never been in a relationship before that was openly acknowledged. Most of the men I've known wanted it to stay hidden."

"Anyone I need to be jealous about?"

"No. Nobody mattered before you."

"I'm glad to hear it." Kearney pulled him close, unbuttoning Ryan's shirt. "And nobody is ever going to matter again." His hands slid inside, possessive on warm skin. "Do you know how long it's been since I even got to touch you?"

"Two weeks." The President was not the only one who had been counting.

"That's right, two damned long weeks, when I've wanted you every single moment of every single day."

"I know." Reciprocal fingers on buttons, on zippers, Ryan's chin lifting as his throat was kissed and bitten and his bandaged hand tussled with tiny fastenings. "I've wanted you, too, just as much."

"You have, huh?" Ryan's shirt fell to the floor, pants and shoes followed. "God, look at you, a messed-up angel. There's stuff I want to do to you that I don't even have a name for."

The awkward hand was making mutual undressing virtually impossible. Frustrated, Kearney stepped back out of his own clothing in seconds, kicked the discarded garments away contemptuously and grabbed Ryan's hand, drawing him into a shallow chair where he sat straddling Kearney's lap, looking down at him in wonderment.

"You know you can do any damned thing you want," the President breathed. "With me or to me. You know that, don't you?"

"Anything?"

"Anything." Hips shifted, legs parted. "They called me in Prague and said you were hurt, and the world fell apart. I knew I had to get back to you so that we could say and do everything we missed out on before. This was never about the physical stuff, Chad. I can get that when I want it. This is about having what I need … and what I need, these days, is you."

Ryan leaned down and kissed him, almost roughly, feeling flesh stir beneath him, feeling the proud chest heave against his.

"You know that Aesop's Fable, 'The Lion and the Mouse'? How the lion was trapped in a net and the mouse gnawed through the ropes to free him? That lion thought he had everything; he was king of the jungle and everybody was afraid of him. Turned out only the mouse was truly his friend. When he needed help, that's who was there for him – the mouse, someone the rest of the world ignored. You saved my life the day you got between me and a madman with a gun, Chad, but you've gone on saving it over and over every day since. I couldn't manage without you. I hope you know that."

Ryan ruffled his fingers through iron-gray hair. "Lion's mane," he said, indulgently. "You'd look magnificent with a beard."

"I'd look ridiculous, trust me." But the words were lost in kisses that became more and more heated; sweat started on Kearney's neck and Chad kissed it down over his collar-bone, easing out of his lap and dropping to his knees on the floor with an expression of mischievous intent in his eyes.

"You know what I want to do?"

"Oh, God, really?" But the way Ryan was licking his lips left no room for doubt.

"Really." The first kiss, almost chaste, was above the navel, the tongue slithering down lasciviously to explore the little hollow, to suck and probe suggestively. "Slide forward." And he positioned Kearney on the very edge of the chair, thighs spread. "I don't want you to do a thing, Doug. Relax. Let it happen. Enjoy it."

"'Relax', he says! Honey, I don't want to relax. What I want is to nail you into the middle of next week."

"Not tonight," was the firm rejoinder. "Tonight, this is all about you."

And the wet mouth opened again, inhaled, took in the rough sweating manhood in a single voluptuous movement. This was what Ryan had been fantasizing about ever since he'd crawled out from under the anesthetic at the hospital; had been thinking about it in detail, in fact, since their very first encounter, but he had preferred to let Kearney set the pace between them. The timing had never felt right before; the almost-shy experimentation, the dexterous use of hands, the frantic friction of tightly-pressed bodies, somehow had seemed everything that was allowed, everything that was possible in their brief and secret windows of opportunity. This was both too committing and too anonymous, the act either of men who understood one another well enough to trust, or who did not know one another at all and did not want to. They had turned away from it almost by mutual consent, and now it was Ryan who made the demand and who manhandled Kearney with an almost-ruthlessness that was a very new thing in their relationship.

Kearney groaned, caught on the edge of need, mind and body conspiring to render him a taut mass of nerves trapped in a physique crying for relief. The soft inside of Ryan's mouth grew slicker and slicker as he slavered on quivering flesh, letting it slide back and forth across his tongue, feeling it scrape in and out of his gullet. He opened further, letting Kearney take what he wanted, sensing the fierce restraint that kept the large hands framing his face but would not permit wanton lunging; letting the rhythm build, letting them both understand that they could do this without loss of dignity, without one of them having to get hurt, without it being abusive. So often it turned into a power exchange, into dominance and submission, into one man wreaking havoc on the other, but this was the surrender of equals; it was smooth, gentle and right. Ryan throated the last thrust as easily as the first, calm as the pulse filled him, receiving without hesitation, stilling as Kearney stilled and listening to the sound of his breathing in the tranquil room.

Doug writhed, withdrawing abruptly, bending to smash ungainly kisses into Chad's salted lips. "So that's how I taste." He slid from the chair and knelt, pulling Ryan into his arms.

"You've never had that?"

"Not from anyone who cared." Kearney kissed him again, pressing him down to the fleecy rug. "I want to do it to you; teach me how."

"I will, but not tonight. It was perfect the way it was; I'd rather sleep, if that's okay?"

"Sleep? You give me the best sucking of my entire life and you want to sleep? What the hell's the matter with you?" And then mock-outrage dissolved into laughter. "Of course you can sleep, honey, if you want, I'm not going to refuse you a damned thing. I feel like I want to give you the world right now, and a box to put it in."

Ryan stumbled to his feet, pulling Kearney with him, steering him to the bed. "I don't want the world," he said. "Just the man who runs it."

"Well, he's yours, too." Kearney settled beside him and hauled the covers around them both. "As long as you want him, which I'm hoping will be a while."

Ryan yawned, burrowing against him, face to the strong chest, arms like steel bands closing around him. "Forever, then?"

"Suits me," replied the President happily. "And maybe even longer."

During the night, in snatches of vivid consciousness, Ryan remembered that he was naked, that Kearney was naked, that the bed was wide and that they were together, touching and being touched as he'd always dreamed they would. In the early morning, with the dawn peeping through the window and sounds of movement beginning around them, they were still side by side; there would be no-one on the establishment by now who did not know that he had spent the night in the President's bed, not one member of staff who could be in doubt about the nature of their relationship.

Ryan rolled towards him. His fingertips brushing Kearney's chin were closely followed by his lips, then by his tongue.

"Scratchy," he observed, not quite half awake.

"Uh-huh." Kearney's limp arms slid around his shoulders and folded him as close as possible without crushing the injured wrist. "Are you trying to seduce me, Colonel?" His tone was the ultimate indulgence, the aural equivalent of warm chocolate sauce.

"Yes, Mr President, I am. Am I likely to succeed?"

There was an upheaval like an earthquake and Kearney wrestled Chad into his arms, rolling him onto his back and settling on top of him. A lock of blond hair had fallen over Ryan's brow, boyish and too long for military protocol; indulgent fingers brushed it back.

"God, Chad," Kearney whispered, his eyes brilliant. "I want to fuck you. I really want to fuck you."

"Go ahead," was the hoarse response. "Don't just talk about it, do it."

And they slid together in a slow, tumbling motion, all hands and breath and lingering glances. It was gentle and dreamlike, slicked fingers pressing into Ryan to prepare for the blunt honesty of insertion. He was crushed against the mattress but rose from it to claim Kearney and pull him in, straining to engulf more and more of him as he pressed forward, frustrated at the limits of mere flesh, hungrily cramming body into body.

"Come on, come on, harder!"

Expletives, orders, instructions barked with passion that was almost anger, fingers clawing Kearney's pale shoulders and firm biceps muscles, gashing the back of his neck and tangling in his hair. Their position should not have been tenable, Ryan's spine twisted, his thighs braced by Kearney's muscular forearms, his erection chafed in the sweat between their bellies, but he didn't care. Somewhere far inside him there was repeated pressure on yearning flesh, forging him into a new shape, hammering beyond the reach of ordinary sensation, sending him into overload, into confusion, into collapse, into the look on Kearney's face as he emptied everything he was into the wantonly receptive body.

Harsh gasps of near exhaustion, and somehow he folded Doug against his chest and soothed him gently. The discomfort of his injuries, which had magically seemed to vanish, now returned to haunt him in full measure, and he wondered if he would ever be able to move without pain again.

"You want to clean up?" Doug's mouth brushed the flat plane of Ryan's breast.

"No. I don't want to get out of bed yet. We'll have to, soon enough."

"True. And we can't ever hope to hide the evidence."

Idly Ryan stroked his neck. "You realize you're completely out of the closet, don't you?"

Kearney snuffled against his chest. "Was I ever really in it? There have always been people who knew."

"There's a difference between knowing and having to know," was the sage response. "Some people might have preferred to pretend it wasn't happening. I'll go along with whatever you want, Doug, but this could end your Presidency."

"I know." Kearney squirmed up the bed to kiss him again, sleepy mouths fastening together in relaxed appreciation. "I just don't know that I care a whole hell of a lot any more."

Opening his eyes a couple of hours later and discovering that he was alone again hardly came as any surprise to Ryan. He had been aware that the other half of the bed was empty, but had been so content that he never thought to question it. Kearney was elsewhere, that was all. There would inevitably be work for him to do and he had slipped out quietly – showered and dressed without a sound and gone, Ryan supposed with a silent chuckle, to run the world.

A gentle knock on the door may not have been the first; perhaps that was what had broken through the fog of sleep. "It's Olivia."

"Come in." He sat up in bed, pulling tumbled bedding around himself, aware from the limited view he had in the dressing-table mirror that no man had ever looked so thoroughly fucked. His hand scrabbled aimlessly at his hair, brought it into line, and he hauled the sheet under his arms until he looked to himself like some nervous teenager waiting for her gynecologist.

Olivia was in jeans and a summer top, a bright explosion of pink and yellow which suited her coloring. She eased around the door like some long-lost sorority sister and had no hesitation in sitting on the bed.

"Dr Franklyn wanted me to ask about your wrist. How is it this morning?"

"Not bad." He was aware of feeling stale and smelling of sex. His clothes from the night before had been piled on a chair – Kearney's doing, obviously – but there could be no dissembling what had occurred. "Where's Doug?"

"In the library. When you're ready, he'd like you to join him. Mitch Booth and General Barrington arrived a while ago; apparently there's some situation developing on the Chinese border, I don't have the details. Anyway the President says you're absolutely to have breakfast first. Would you like me to bring it here?"

"You shouldn't wait on me," he exclaimed, feeling a stab of guilt. "Don't you have things to do?"

"Not this morning," she grinned. "Why don't you sit back and enjoy it?"

But in the end he retreated to his own room and showered and breakfasted there, scrambling awkwardly into polo shirt and jeans and having Olivia re-tie the sling for his wrist. When she was done she looked him up and down in approval.

"I know you're happy," she said. "It's right there in your eyes." And she threw both arms around his neck and hugged him impulsively. "Come on, now, I'll escort you downstairs to the President."

Kearney was sitting at a table in the library, turned sideways to the door as he peered into a computer screen. On a couch under the window were Booth and Barrington, their carefully casual jeans and checked shirts somehow wildly out of place. The coffee table in front of them held a litter of papers and satellite surveillance photographs and to judge from the position of the empty cups, the President had only just vacated the chair opposite.

"Good morning." Ryan spoke to the room in general, uncomfortably aware that Olivia had abandoned him in the doorway and returned to whatever other duties might have been assigned her.

"Morning." Booth and Barrington greeted him breezily. Kearney bounded out of his seat and looked as if he might be on the verge of leaping across to embrace him, but settled for one of his lop-sided smiles and a slightly abashed expression in his eyes.

"Hey," he said, softly.

"Hey." Ryan returned the informal greeting. "What's happening?"

"It's Holofernes, the Kyrgyz end." Kearney indicated the VDU screen. "It's on fire." Leaning closer, Ryan could see rapidly-refreshing pictures of the plant with a plume of smoke pouring out along the prevailing wind. "They're not making any attempt to extinguish it, and we can't understand why. What's more, they're not allowing anyone to leave. Half an hour ago, some vehicles pulled up that we thought were fire trucks, but when we look closer they're tanks enforcing the perimeter – anybody who tries to get out gets shot. It looks as if they're going to let the plant burn and everybody in it. Military, civilians, the whole lot."

"Do we have anyone inside?"

"No, but that doesn't mean our allies didn't – we're not the only country in the world with intelligence capabilities, after all. I've got a video conference with Howard and the CIA coming up; I want you to sit in."

"Sure," Ryan nodded.

"Good. George, take a look at this, will you ... " And Kearney turned away, preoccupied, and gave his full attention to the task at hand.

Several minutes later, they repaired to the communications post in the sun room, where the video conference had been set up. The room held one large table surrounded by chairs, and along one wall a bank of view screens displayed a variety of information. One held the rigid features of the Vice President, another streamed video of the fire, a third displayed the satellite weather picture, and the fourth contained the image of a severe, thin-faced African American man in a sharp suit – Brent McArdle, Director of the CIA. This was Ryan's first encounter with him.

"Gentlemen." Kearney sat, gesturing for the others to do so. "Brent, what are you hearing about the fire?"

McArdle cleared his throat. "Mr President, my sources indicate sabotage, although I have no firm information who's responsible; my people are having meetings throughout the intelligence community and I hope to be able to give you something shortly. Meanwhile, if you're asking for a gut reaction ... " He paused, waiting for Kearney to respond.

"Go on."

"Sir, only one of our immediate partners has so far failed to ask whether we started it. I take that to indicate they know for sure we didn't, which may be because they did. On that basis, my hunch is we'll find French Secret Service at the bottom of this mess somewhere."

"Motive being?"

McArdle shrugged. "Bad feeling between Paris and Beijing since the One China Policy; France sold weapons to Taiwan, China closed the French consulate in Guangzhou. Governments don't forget things like that, and the same satellite information that we get is also available to the French. It's not much, but if they had men on the ground already ... "

" ... they might have decided to go in when we stayed out. If that's the case, they should have informed us what they were doing."

"Yes, sir, they should. But you know as well as I do, Mr President, that sometimes it's easier just to apologize afterwards."

"Yeah," Kearney nodded. "No doubt that will come as a great consolation to all the guys burning to death in there. Howard, recommendations?"

"No, sir, not one. The plant is on Kyrgyz sovereign territory and as far as we know there are no US or other foreign nationals involved. We have no leverage in this case; all we can do is offer to help them fight their fire. They'll say they've got it under control, and then they'll sit and watch it burn. We can't stop it, I'm afraid."

Kearney groaned, passing a hand across his eyes. "What do they have stashed in there that they don't want us to know about?"

"Warheads," rejoined McArdle, crisply. "It's the only thing that makes any sense. They've been illegally stockpiling them for the Chinese, and they probably have rail-mounted launch facilities, too. It's what I would do. But if they let people out now, there's no way they can contain either the radiation or the information; they don't have adequate decontamination facilities to process everybody – and frankly it's cheaper for them if they don't. So they'll wait for the flames to go out, pour a million tons of concrete over the site and pretend it never happened. These guys are playing a long game, Mr President, and they've never objected to human sacrifice on a massive scale if they thought the situation justified it. Don't forget the June Fourth Massacre; they killed at least a thousand of their own people then."

"So, you're saying this is collateral damage? They budgeted for it?"

"Pretty much. People are infinitely replaceable; only ideals matter."

Unexpectedly, it was Maddocks who intervened to break the appalled silence that followed this remark. "What we need to be concerned about, Mr President, is the weather. If you'll look at your chart, you'll see that prevailing winds will take the smoke into the mountains. That area has a population density of less than three people per square mile and the toxic gases will disperse without killing more than a few goats and buzzards. On the other hand if the wind changes we could be looking at an ecological disaster, and we may need to think about lodging some kind of protest on environmental grounds. There are always NGOs in the area monitoring pollution; we can route it through one of them if necessary."

"You're seriously recommending no action?" Kearney leaned back in his chair and regarded the screens calmly. "Both of you?"

"No action, sir."

Abruptly the President stood. "All right. Brief me if the weather changes. Thank you, gentlemen." He strode briskly from the conference table leaving Barrington and Booth, nonplussed, to continue the discussion without him.

Ryan, unsure where he belonged, hesitated a moment before following Kearney from the room. He caught up with him outside, leaning on the top rail of the horse paddock watching the animals frisk energetically in the morning light.

"My mom loved this place," Kearney said in a conversational tone as he drew close. "I always hoped I could buy it back for her one day, but she died before I got the chance. I'm still hoping to own it again some time, to bring it into the family where it belongs."

"It's so peaceful." Ryan watched the parade of emotions crossing the other man's face. "Serene. I can see how coming here would make you feel stronger."

"Yes. It's like a prayer or a piece of music; it seems to set everything right."

Ryan slid an arm around his shoulders. "I don't understand," he admitted, "how the sun can be shining, and the sky can be blue, while a democratically-elected government is watching its own people burn to death and not doing a damn thing to stop it."

"It doesn't make sense, does it?" Kearney sighed and reached for his hand. "You're happy, you're in love, you don't see why anyone should have to suffer? That's it, isn't it?"

"It is. I'm not going to apologize for it."

"You shouldn't, it's who you are." Kearney drew him closer, so that they stood side-by-side leaning on the rail and watching the horses. No scene could have been further removed from the hell currently raging under that far distant mountain-scape. "But there are things we can change and things we can't. The tough part is learning to tell the difference."

"You get this a lot, don't you?" During the hours of darkness, Ryan had done his best to forget that this man's importance extended beyond the boundaries of his own country, that half the world looked to him for solutions while the other half knew he was the cause of its problems. Now it was being borne in upon him with horrible clarity, and he was able to recognize the source of Kearney's need for intimacy, to touch and to be touched, to find something personal and reliable that could never be tainted by politics. "People die when you could save them but you aren't allowed to try. Damn, I can't imagine what it must be like to be so powerful and at the same time so ... so impotent. And you're too sensitive to block it out; those people are part of you, you're part of them. You're feeling what they feel, right along with them, right now."

"That's how it is," agreed Kearney. "Credit for the good stuff goes to the guys who do the work, but I get the blame for whatever goes wrong. The buck stops here." He flattened one hand across his ribcage. "'*The toad beneath the harrow knows exactly where each tooth-point goes*'. It gets no easier, but to have someone to share it with who actually understands ... " He paused, taking a long, deep breath of clean country air. "Welcome to my world, honey," the President told him sadly.

For the next two hours, nothing changed. The monitor showed the same deathly pictures; clouds of gray, the occasional lick of flames, vehicles coming and going, no attempt to fight the fire. Berry looked in briefly, exchanged cursory greetings with her father and obtained permission to hike a nearby trail with Olivia, Dr Franklyn and a couple of the local agents. She vanished again before he had fully registered her presence, and he returned to brooding uselessly on the situation.

After the third hour, however, he drew himself together with a massive effort of will.

"Chad, let's get the guys and take the bike over to the Lowman House. There's nothing we can do here; Howard can monitor things on my behalf. George, Mitch, you'll stick around and have lunch with us?"

"Thank you, sir." It was Booth who spoke.

"Call me if you need me," continued Kearney decisively. "I'll come right back." And a few minutes later they were out in the woods.

The big Honda 750 was not ideally suited for narrow woodland trails. Kearney wrestled it for an hour along pathways mostly used by forest workers, thrashing out his remaining frustrations and ultimately bringing it to a halt under a canopy of trees at the lip of a rise, bracing the bike with his feet and easing the engine to an idle. He was in jeans, sneakers and tee-shirt; plastered to his back, sweat and dust almost bonding them together, was Ryan. They wore identical baseball caps lettered 'FBI' in white. Ryan's left arm was wrapped around Kearney's waist and in his left hand he gripped the thick belt Kearney wore, anchoring himself in place.

"They keep trying to make me wear a helmet," the President said. "It's the law in this state, and my guys all panic about what would happen if anybody ever got a photo of me riding without, but so long as I'm on my own land I'm damned if I'm going to wear one."

"Fine in theory." Ryan's chin was on his shoulder and his left thumb soothed back and forth across the taut flatness of the man's stomach. "Right up until the moment you fall off."

"I don't intend to fall off."

Kearney looked thoughtfully over a verdant shelf of land stretching to the eastward, which even with his limited knowledge of agriculture Chad could tell would be productive dairy country. A few yards away a second bike halted, its riders suitably helmeted; one of the local agents and a member of the Presidential football team had remained within a discreet perimeter the whole time.

"Well, this is the Lowman House – my house, the one Kirsten hates. I must admit, it's had a sad history; my mother's cousin Harold took three years to die of wounds he got in Korea, and eighteen months after that his father took a shotgun out to the barn and blew his own head off. That left Great Aunt Martha on her own and she couldn't run the place by herself, so she let out the grazing and just stayed on in the house until it fell apart. It's barely been touched since the sixties. I did work on it whenever I could, but it's like trying to catch the sea in a bucket. The place needs major investment, and when I had the time I didn't have the money. But as it turned out, Martha and I outlived everybody else in the family; when she died, five or six years ago, I inherited the house and everything in it. I had a crew come in and weatherproof it, but it'll be years before it's fit to live in."

"This is your project?" The hand left Kearney's belt and burrowed under his tee-shirt to spread across his chest; fingertips flicked a nipple and moved on, exploring until Kearney's hand clamped down and held Ryan's fingers in place through the shirt.

"What do you think?"

He sighed. "It's beautiful. Sheltered, private, and the air ... "

"I know. I wish I could bottle it and take it back to the city. And you should see the place in winter; it's like being in a Christmas card. I spent my summers here as a kid, running wild with horses and dogs and swimming in the lake; it may not be where I grew up, but to me this is my childhood home. This is the place where I feel most like myself. And when the country finally gets tired of me, this is where I'm going to retire to. I want to live here and put the house back together with my own hands. Only nowadays ... " He faltered, then continued more strongly. "Nowadays, more and more, I find I'm thinking about you being here with me. On a permanent basis."

"Really?" Astonished, delighted, half afraid, Ryan sought to turn aside the demons with a joke. "You really think you could stand having me around on a permanent basis?"

"Think?" Kearney echoed, bewildered. "I know. It was obvious right from the start, wasn't it? To both of us, I mean."

He still had not turned. He was looking over the little valley, at the pale wood of the old house, at the half-ruined barn beside it, at the dark lines of fences and the green mass of the forest, obviously seeing nothing but a place inside his head that would be empty and unattractive without Chad Ryan to share it.

"You're asking me to marry you," he said, in case the implications should have escaped either of them.

"I guess so."

A long, long pause then, while the breeze danced softly around them, caressing their hair, soothing their brows. And suddenly, between one heartbeat and the next, the almost inaudible response.

"Then I guess I'm going to have to accept your offer. Of course I am, Doug. Of course."

9.

Lunch was a subdued affair. For the first half of the meal, people repeatedly rose from the table to check the situation with Holofernes, but by the mid-way point a general air of despondency had settled on them. It was, after all, the middle of the night in Kyrgyzstan and – as clear as their pictures were – there was little to be gained from examining a constant satellite feed of flames and smoke against a backdrop of dark sky. For Kearney, with his fire-fighter's experience, it was particularly frustrating; had he still been commanding his own ladder company he would have known exactly what to do and how to set about it, although he was the first to admit the utter futility of attempting to stem any conflagration on so staggering a scale. The immediacy of the pictures and the impossibility of intervening from such a distance, however, combined to render him the most useless of spectators, not a role for which he was ideally suited. There were no decisions being required of him and although he strove to put the matter out of his mind and concentrate on things more immediate and remediable, the effort it cost was plentifully apparent to those around him.

"I need to talk to you, Chad." Booth cornered him as they disbanded after the meal, the President and General Barrington a few steps ahead along the hallway. Bright sunlight poured through the windows; the day was blue and gold and shining. Ryan stopped and turned back. "When you guys get home I want you to have the security briefing for family members. You need to be aware, Chad; enough people know about your relationship with the President for you to be a potential kidnap victim … or even an assassination target in your own right."

"What?" Ryan regarded the older man as though he was spouting the most arrant nonsense.

"We were lucky the other day; if the guy you ran into had been an international terrorist he'd have taken you out in a heartbeat. You must realize that anybody who wants a way of hurting Doug now has the opportunity to do it through you. That automatically gives you the same security status as Kirsten or Berry, and if I wouldn't let the First Lady wander around the city on her own – and I sure as hell wouldn't – I'm damned if I'll let you. Your life isn't your own any more. You're part of him now."

"I know."

"Wouldn't have it any other way, huh?"

"No."

"No. Well, that makes it easier." Mitch turned, glancing to where the other two once more had their heads bowed over the computer screen. "Did he ask you?"

"Yes." And somehow it was no surprise that he had already known.

"I thought he would. You said 'no', of course?"

"Of course." An ironic chuckle. "It never occurred to me there could be so much form-filling and protocol in any relationship."

Mitch laughed. "If that's a problem, maybe you'd better find another guy."

"All right. Next Presidential assassination I'm involved in, I'll try to spend some time interviewing candidates."

"Round about the time Hell freezes over, I take it?"

"About that time," was the firm response. "Not a moment before."

"Good man." Mitch gripped Ryan's arm and steered him to the corner. "I need you to do something," he said, "and not to ask questions about it until later."

"What sort of thing?"

Mitch glanced along the hallway. "Ask me to stay. When George leaves, ask me to stay for the afternoon. Make any excuse you like, as long as he goes and I don't."

Ryan's eyes flickered nervously in Barrington's direction. "What about the President ... ?"

"Don't say anything. Not a word. It'll make sense, I promise, but you're gonna have to trust me for now. Oh, and it would really help if you could be kind of gay about asking, too."

"I don't ... "

"It's not that I'd call George a homophobe exactly, but let's just say he's not the most sympathetic of men when it comes to alternative lifestyles. Make it sound like you want to discuss paint chips and fabric samples and he'll run a mile."

Ryan glanced from the President to Mitch and back again. It was potentially a difficult moment; the thought of doing anything – even as apparently innocent as this – without clearing it with Kearney first, was quite alien. Nevertheless he reminded himself that he would never have got close to Kearney in the first place if not for this man. Mitch had known the President a long time; if he had ever intended to harm him, he could have accomplished it easily enough without involving Ryan.

"You know what?" He raised his voice a little and gripped the man's arm with every indication of enthusiasm. "Why don't you come and see for yourself? And wait till you see the drawings, it's going to be spectacular. That would be okay, Doug, wouldn't it?"

Kearney had turned back and was regarding the pair of them with a puzzled expression. "I'm sorry?"

"I was telling Mitch about our plans for the house, but maybe he should just take a look at it? He could travel back with us this evening, couldn't he?"

Kearney shrugged. "I guess, if he wants to. How about that, Mitch?"

"Love to." The tone of voice was tolerant rather than enthusiastic, a nicely-judged touch of unwilling martyrdom.

"George, you in? There's not a lot more any of us can do here, after all."

"Thank you, sir," was the cool response, "but I'll pass if you don't mind. I should be getting back to DC to liaise with the Vice President and Director McArdle."

"Yeah, George, you go on ahead." Booth clapped him on the shoulder. "I'll catch up with you later this evening; you can fill me in on the details then."

Barrington glanced at Ryan, at the floor, then back at Booth. "Looking forward to it," he said, and turned to resume his conversation with the President.

"Not bad," Booth said, as he rejoined Ryan.

"You're going to explain all this, aren't you?"

"A couple of hours from now, I absolutely guarantee it. Guess we'll have to go and walk round this house of yours in the meantime, though, just to make it look real. Don't suppose that'll break your heart, will it?"

Ryan shook his head. "Probably not," he admitted. "Although I'm convinced Doug thinks I've gone mad."

"If he does," was the quiet response, "he's doing a good job of hiding it. In fact, Chad, all things considered, I'd say he was taking it rather well."

Barrington took his departure shortly afterwards, heading for the airport and a scheduled flight back to DC, and within minutes the other three piled into the back of the armored Cherokee and set off by road for the Lowman House, not nearly so direct or interesting as journey as the one Ryan and the President had taken by motorcycle on the previous day. Nor was the weather quite as co-operative as it had been then; although the sun was still shining benevolently, a cold northerly breeze had sprung up and was scything down the valley towards them as they got out of the car.

"My grandmother used to call that a 'lazy wind'," observed Booth. "It doesn't take the long way round, it goes right through you. Is this where you're going to establish your library, Mr President?"

"No. I want the Ford House for that, if my lawyers can ever hammer out a deal with the estate. This place is too far off the beaten track, and anyway I'd rather have it as a home. Chad, d'you want to take a look inside?"

"What? Oh, yes, why not?"

One of the Secret Service guys was already disabling alarms, and moments later they were inside the greenish, slightly decaying interior of what had been a modestly elegant house, empty now of all furniture and effects, the haunt of spiders and silence.

"Everything's in storage," Kearney informed Ryan as he put his head around the doorway into a room that boasted a stone fireplace and empty oak shelves from floor to ceiling. "After Kirsten decided she didn't like it here, I knew I wasn't going to be able to get back for a while so I had it all packed and shipped to a facility in Burlington. This is the first time

I've seen it since it was emptied out. Berry swears the place is haunted," he added. "I'm beginning to understand what she means. It is kind of creepy like this."

Ryan shrugged. "It's just cold and unloved," he said, "as if it knows it's been rejected. Nothing a few cans of paint wouldn't cure."

Kearney was watching him, a kind of proprietorial satisfaction in his gaze. "You're ready to jump right in and start, aren't you?"

"Whenever you say the word. This house needs somebody to take care of it."

There was more that he could have said, more that he would have liked to say, but he was too aware of Mitch, the security guys, the football officer no more than a dozen paces from the President's side.

"We'd need to have a lot of stuff installed if we wanted to stay overnight," murmured Kearney. "Communications stuff." He paused. "Electricity. Water. The plumbing's ... mostly of historic interest."

"And you're surprised Kirsten hated it?"

"She didn't hate it. She just didn't appreciate it the way I do. We had oil lamps here when I was growing up. They made the shadows come to life. Looking back on it now, I'd say it was kind of romantic."

"It sounds wonderful," said Ryan. "Like an adventure."

"It was," said the President. "It could be again."

"So who's doing the haunting?" Mitch asked, abruptly, one large hand thumping down firmly onto an acorn newel at the foot of the wide stairs. The sound re-echoed through the house. "Martha? Harold? Henry?"

"Martha'd never dream of haunting anyone," laughed Kearney. "She didn't have an ax to grind with a soul, living or dead. Nor did Harold. Henry would have been an angry ghost, but I doubt it's him either. If there's anybody here, my money's on Gran'pa Herbert. He built the place, after all."

"Berry didn't tell you who it was?"

"Berry didn't know," came the answer. "Just that there was a presence here. But whoever it was, she wasn't afraid of them." Then, more quietly. "Mitch, why don't you wait in the car? I want to show Chad upstairs."

"Glad to. Just be careful, okay? I don't want to have to explain to the Vice President that I let the pair of you fall through a rotten floor."

Kearney smiled at him. "Hey, I'm the one who's supposed to be afraid of the Vice President," he said, grabbing a flash-light proffered by one of the agents. It looked as if it and a couple of its buddies would have been more than capable of illuminating the average rock concert.

"I hate to disagree with you, Mr President," returned Ryan, allowing himself to be escorted up the stairs and into the echoing darkness of the upper story, "but I don't think there's anybody in the country who isn't afraid of the Vice President, and that includes me. So maybe we'd better try not to upset him, if that's okay?"

"That's my Chad," joked Kearney, sliding an arm around him as soon as they were out of sight of the others. "All the backbone of a wet sponge."

"Not really." And in a secretive patch of darkness at the top of the stairs Ryan held still for a moment and allowed himself to be kissed, briefly, possessively, matter-of-factly. "I just like to be able to choose my battles, if I can."

"Yeah," agreed Kearney, "that sounds like a damned good idea. I wish I had the opportunity to choose mine. You want to tell me what all that business was about inviting Mitch to stay? I've never heard you putting on an act like that before; you sounded like something out of '*Torch Song Trilogy*'."

"I've been promised a full explanation," was the quiet reply. "Something to do with getting General Barrington out of the way, I think."

"Hmmm. I wasn't going to say anything but I have an idea Berry was kind of marched off the premises, too. She's never been all that keen on hiking and countryside stuff; I got the impression today's little expedition was more Olivia's idea than hers. Mind you, it's also possible somebody was expecting the shit to hit the fan on Holofernes and they didn't want Berry getting in the way or distracting my attention. The problem with my job is that you never quite know when you're being manipulated – and you never really know who's doing it. Not until afterwards, and then only if you're lucky."

"Are you worried?"

Kearney's eyebrows rose. "That's a damned good question," he conceded. "As a matter of fact, I can't work out whether I should be or not. This is one of those times when you have to trust that the guys around you are doing their jobs, but I won't deny there's an itchy feeling between my shoulder-blades. Still, we should be thinking about more positive things." He threw open a door onto a room which still managed to be light despite the shutters over the windows. "This will be our bedroom."

It had obviously been magnificent once: a tiled fireplace between two wide windows; the remnant of what was probably extremely expensive hand-blocked wallpaper; the bed would go just so, and there was a shadow on one wall where a huge wardrobe had apparently stood for several decades.

"We could turn the dressing-room into a bathroom; it's small but it should just about work."

Kearney stood in the doorway, letting Ryan explore. Not that there was much to see; fallen soot on the hearth, nail-marks in the floorboards where an unsympathetic modern carpet had been tacked in the fifties, caked-up paint obscuring the details of the window-frames. It smelled dry, dusty, neglected.

"Our bedroom?"

They were words which somehow didn't work together. It was too soon, too much and although he could envisage a future unfolding with this man, Ryan was wondering why on Earth it had to happen now, what was so vitally important about starting it immediately when the reality was that Kearney would be needed elsewhere for months, maybe even years to come.

"Unless you hate it. There are five more, but this is the biggest ... and it has the best views. I thought maybe you could ... take over co-ordinating the project, getting crews in to sort out the basics, liaise with security and architects and see it through the Act 250 permit process. I never had anyone to share this stuff with before."

Ryan was watching him carefully. "Are you afraid I'll leave you?"

The thought had struck him with sudden, shattering clarity. This frantic long-term planning, the desperate search for permanence, these were the products of inbuilt insecurity on an awe-inspiring scale – and all in the man the world's most powerful nation had chosen to safeguard its future. It was astonishing that any President could ever be so unsure of himself; how could a facade of such massive confidence have been assembled on such shaky foundations? And what, he wondered, was his role supposed to be in maintaining the edifice? Running repairs? Or would he be responsible for the full-scale underpinning of an otherwise dangerously decrepit structure?

"Maybe. Maybe not."

"Was that why you made me promise?" Now that Ryan thought about it, there had been more than a trace of affliction in the suddenness of the proposal. Not that the knowledge affected the nature of his answer, except to make him even more certain of it.

"It could be." The ambiguous response was pitched somewhere between a child's truculence and a politician's maddening evasiveness.

"Are you trying to bribe me into staying by promising me treats and toys?" It was an unworthy thought, but one Ryan was unable to resist.

"I don't want to lose you, that's all."

"And you think you might?"

Kearney shrugged, his frame seeming shrunken somehow, as if a weight had settled on his shoulders that had not been there yesterday and that he could not readily shrug away.

"I have to make some tough choices," he said. "Sometimes that alienates people. People who think it's simple. It isn't."

"I've never believed any of it was simple." Ryan fell silent for a moment. "We're not talking about the house here, are we?"

"No. Lives. Deaths. It's what they employ me for, Chad, to carry that stuff around so they don't have to."

"I know. You're a man of sorrows, aren't you? One who carries the weight of all the sin in the world. '*A man of sorrows, and acquainted with grief*.'"

"I might have known you'd see it like that. I knew you'd get it, and I knew you'd be the only one who would. You could never believe anything bad of me, could you, honey? You'd fight in my corner even if

I didn't. One of these days, you're going to be the very last friend I have."

Ryan was shivering now, and it was nothing to do with the temperature in the room. "Somebody walked over my grave," he said, lifting his eyes to the President's all-too-knowing gaze.

Kearney smiled wanly. "Was it me?" A feeble attempt to lighten the mood.

"No," came the sombre response. "I think it was both of us."

They wandered around the old property for a further half-hour, battling with a rolled-up collection of drawings that seemed to bear little resemblance to the structure as it existed, discussing drainage and garden features and the size of the garage, arguing over the numbers of staff who would be permitted to share their establishment. They were not men brought up to luxury and both of them were more than adequately equipped to fend for themselves, but the simple fact was that no President could live a wholly secluded life, even in retirement. He would entertain, he would write, he would engage in charitable works, and while he might well be permitted to dig his own garden or even paint his own front door if the mood took him, society as a whole and the tabloid press in particular would never forgive him if he cooked his own meals or washed his own socks. However competent he may have been in his previous existence, he was now condemned to the life of an exhibit in a museum; he was required to be decorative, interesting, but certainly not functional.

"It'll drive me mad," Kearney said, looking up at the remains of a shingled roof covered in several layers of blue tarp. "They're going to have to find a security detail who can climb up there with me – and they'd damned well better be prepared to do more than just pass me the nails."

Mitch was leaning against the car. "You could pay people to do that a hundred times over," he observed, unsympathetically.

"That's not the point. The point is that it's my family's house, and I owe it my individual care. That's important to me."

"You're eccentric," said Mitch. "You know that? Chad, are you going to let him get away with this kind of stuff?"

"I think," said Ryan, as he slid into the back seat and waited for Kearney's large bulk to fill up the space next to him, looking fondly into the man's world-weary eyes as he did so, "my role in this is to let him get away with any little thing he wants."

As they glided up the drive to the Ford house, however, the mood of jaunty optimism vanished on the breeze. A dark limousine was prominently parked out front, and the smile vanished from Mitch's face as he set eyes on it.

"Well," he said, "I guess that's the end of the fun for today. Chad, you're about to get that explanation I promised you. Just bear in mind when you listen to it that I didn't really have a choice."

They stepped inside the hallway to be greeted by the looming, ominous figure of a man who by rights should have been several hundred miles away from where he was. Ryan's first impression of CIA Director Brent McArdle was that he was taller than he appeared on the TV screen. Very much taller. In fact, now that he was no longer confined to a small electronic box it was apparent he was an impressive six-feet-four, by quite a stretch the tallest man in the room, and packed considerable nervous energy into his lean frame. His dark eyes were steady on the President but gave the appearance of being everywhere at once, as if he was capable of extraordinary multiple focus. There would be little that eluded his attention.

"Brent? What the hell? Aren't you supposed to be in DC?" Automatically, their feet took them into the library, the de facto substitute for the Oval Office.

"No, Mr President, as a matter of fact I've been down the road in Burlington all the time, holed up at the Holiday Inn." McArdle glanced up. "Mitch, good to see you. Colonel Ryan, I'm sorry we're meeting in such circumstances."

"Circumstances?" Ryan repeated numbly.

McArdle looked around. The agents at the entrance quietly closed the doors and stayed outside.

"Doug," said Mitch, "I think we should sit." His tone would have been more than enough to introduce a note of alarm into the room, had McArdle's presence not already done so.

"Is it Kirsten? Has something happened to her?"

"Sir," McArdle assured him, "your family are safe. Every one of them. But it's my duty to advise you that General Barrington was killed soon after he left here this afternoon." The words were carefully and distinctly enunciated, as if in a deliberate attempt to avoid ambiguity.

Kearney crashed ungracefully onto the couch. Ryan said quietly; "Should I leave?"

"No, Colonel." The CIA man seemed to have taken control of the meeting and seated himself opposite the President. Mitch brought over the desk chair. Ryan, lacking other options, dropped into the place beside Doug.

Kearney's mouth set in an obdurate line. "The fact that you're here and telling me this," he said, "presupposes it wasn't an accident."

McArdle's lips pursed. "Sir," he said, bluntly, "it was not. His vehicle was in collision with a logging truck. It was crushed under fifty tons of softwood. His driver," he added, without a flicker of emotion, "escaped with only minor injuries."

"Fortunate." The tone was both sepulchral and disbelieving.

Ryan stared at Mitch. "'Ask me to stay'," he quoted, his insides roiling with uncertainty. "'Make any excuse as long as he goes and I don't'. That's what all that was about? You knew this was going to happen; that's why you didn't want to leave when he did. You made me your accomplice. I wouldn't have done it if I'd known."

"I know that, Chad. I'm sorry."

The room fell silent for a long moment, and suddenly everyone was looking at the President. "Did I order it?" he asked at last.

"Not yet, sir." McArdle's words could almost have been facetious, the set-up for a joke in particularly execrable taste, had it not been for their cryogenic temperature. "But I'm hoping you will."

"Is this supposed to be a coup? Am I Gorbachev in 1991? Is this where I wake up to find tanks in Lafayette Square? "

McArdle took a breath, let it out slowly, let some of the tension seep from his shoulders. "No, sir, nothing of the sort. However I do have evidence that General Barrington engineered the deaths of our agents in Kyrgyzstan on behalf of the People's Republic of China. The Chairman of the Joint Chiefs was a traitor to this country, Mr President. There was no way he could have been put on trial. Our only safe option was to remove him from the picture completely."

"You're telling me this was CIA hit? On US soil?" The tone was less outraged than defeated, infinitely weary, as if this should have been a shocking revelation but somehow it was not.

"Yes. It was carried out by staff from our field office in Montreal, agents with established cover in the logging business. For all intents and purposes, this was an accident between a logger and an unmarked Government car. In due course, our driver will be found guilty of DUI, he'll vanish into the prison system and as far as anybody knows that'll be the end of it. Everyone else will be back in Canada within the hour, Mr President. I'm asking you not to do anything to prevent that."

"Explain it to me," challenged Kearney, combatively. "Tell me why I should listen to a thing you say."

"I'll try, sir." McArdle moved forward in his seat, clasping his hands in front of him in a gesture that usually signified earnestness. It would have been deceptively easy to take him at face value, had he not devoted his life to the covert machinations of the intelligence community. Nevertheless there was something about the reluctance with which he spoke that carried its own conviction. "We became aware several months ago that somebody in the White House itself was passing highly confidential information to Beijing. The quality of data being traded made it possible to eliminate suspicion of anyone below a certain clearance level, and the fact that CIA-only data was never leaked indicated that the source was outside the agency. That was why I took point on the investigation." McArdle paused, looking around at his audience. "You'll be relieved to learn, Mr President, that Colonel Flanagan's health is not nearly as bad as you were led to believe, although he should certainly be taking better care of his diet. It was necessary to remove him and bring in a replacement with no prior connection to anyone on your staff."

"He was a suspect?"

"He was. Although not a strong one, and now completely exonerated. If you wanted to bring him back ... " McArdle paused. "Well, maybe not."

"Me," said Chad. "I was the 'replacement with no prior connection'."

"Yes. You were the right man in the right place as far as we were concerned. Mitch here encouraged the President to offer you a job simply because none of us knew you. We wanted to start over with a clean slate."

"You wanted a harmless non-entity, and that's exactly what I was."

"Chad!"

But McArdle was looking directly at him, eyes like black lasers dissecting him layer by layer.

"I'm not sure I would have expressed it that way, Colonel, but essentially it's true. We needed a place-holder and as far as we were concerned it could have been the guy who cleans the latrines at Quantico. But you turned out better than we expected." He glanced at the President. "Sir, I have no right to pass comment on your private life and I don't intend to do so, but I do want to assure you that none of my investigations have ever shown up anything to Colonel Ryan's discredit. What you have here is an honest and hard-working officer. The circumstances of his recruitment are not his fault and I hope you won't hold them against him. It would be wrong of me not to make that point."

"Thank you." Numbly, Doug patted Chad's arm.

"So, when the Vice President showed me the details of Holofernes ... ?" Ryan's mind was spinning eccentrically, the gears misaligning, the mechanism out of balance and almost juddering to a halt.

"It was to see how you'd react," put in Mitch. "If you'd been involved in anything prejudicial to national security, that would have been your cue but you did nothing. Nor did you when you were asked to liaise with the Vice President. We gave you enough rope to hang yourself but you didn't take it. You just did your job. I may be wrong, but I'm assuming you probably had other things on your mind at the time."

Horrified, Ryan looked down. "I have no desire to act against the interests of the President," he said, more calmly than he felt, acutely aware that the others were exchanging glances over his bowed head. "I never have. I never could."

"The President," the CIA man repeated. "Not the country. Interesting, but I guess personal loyalty is better than no loyalty at all."

"It's fine," said Booth. "We all serve here for different reasons and some of them don't exactly stand up to scrutiny. It doesn't stop us doing our duty."

"No, it does not. Sir," continued McArdle, "ultimately there were only two possible sources for the leak, both highly placed inside the White House, one an elected official and the other an appointee. Either one working in the interests of a foreign power would have been disastrous, not just for the United States but for the entire world. The matter was fully investigated by a task force comprising the Vice President, National Security Advisor and Director, CIA. There have to be checks and balances, Mr President; in this case, that was the three of us."

"Checks and balances?" Kearney got up and walked to the window, turning his back to the company. He seemed to be looking towards the horse paddock, to the driveway along which Berry and her small entourage were even now returning exhausted to the house. "You mean me," he breathed, struggling to process the implications. "I'm the 'elected official'. You thought it might be me."

McArdle, too, rose, apparently in no mood to dissemble. "We did."

Kearney was shaking his head. "So, how did you ... ?"

"Test the hypothesis? There were two pairs of agents with orders to destroy Holofernes from the Kyrgyz end, and each of you was told about one of them. We knew one pair would be betrayed. The men we told you about, sir, completed their task. The other pair ... " He left the sentence hanging.

"Wait." Ryan scrambled upright. "You knew there was a plan to destroy Holofernes? We had people in there?"

"Of course we did," Kearney admitted, coldly. "Of course I knew." He paused, his eyes wandering over Ryan's face as if he thought he might be seeing it for the last time. "Our guys have been part of the train crew ferrying supplies into the tunnel ever since the first sod was cut. Or did you really imagine that we don't have our own suicide bombers? That's a sweet, innocent world you live in, honey; I wish I shared it."

They were staring at one another.

"This was what we were talking about, at the other house?" Ryan asked. "This was what you were struggling with then?"

"It wasn't a struggle," said Kearney. "It wasn't even a choice. If you can't live with that you need to leave, because that's who I am and it's what I do. I'm a widow-maker. It's what they pay me for."

Appalled, Ryan could only watch the way the shutters were falling behind the President's eyes, the way he was methodically arming himself against pain. In stolen moments, he had seen the other Douglas Kearney, the ordinary man he had been; now, in this room, he faced the product left behind when duty and sacrifice had finished making their demands. There was nothing recognizably human there. He was looking at an empty house.

"Mr President," he said, quietly, "may I have your permission to withdraw?"

"This is not my meeting." The response was unusually crisp. "Ask Brent."

Wounded, Ryan turned. "Mr Director?"

"Dismissed, Colonel." McArdle was obviously in no mood to prolong the scene any longer than was absolutely necessary.

"Thank you, sir."

Without a word Ryan turned and made his way out of the room. He was not remotely tempted to glance behind him as he left.

10.

They were wheels-up from Burlington at the hour that on the previous evening had been reserved for sunset and desserts and delighting in one another's company. Now they were in different and not necessarily parallel worlds. Berry, leaning heavily against Ryan, was asleep almost before the pre-flight checks had been completed; the two of them had bagged the rearmost forward-facing double seat and occupied it together without reference to the rest of the party. Kearney, across the aisle, had a single seat and a bundle of papers to share it with; Booth and McArdle, who did not seem to be talking much either, were up in front with the doctor and the rest of the agents. The atmosphere was at best subdued, at worst towards the grim end of purposeful; word of Barrington's death had spread quickly, had hit the wire services as a tragic accident, and those not in the know were deeply distressed by the futility of his loss. Ryan simply did not know what it would be appropriate for him to feel and doubted that, after everything that had happened, he would have had the energy left for any great emotion had he known; thus it was not difficult to simulate an outward despondency when there was nothing but emptiness inside.

His arm was round Berry's shoulders. He smoothed the tangled ends of her hair and wondered if it were always like this with the children of the famous; that they grew up trusting staff and aides and turning to them for comfort because a busy mother or father would always have more urgent priorities than a weary child. Not that Berry understood a tenth of what had taken place, but she knew that her father and his friend were at odds and in those circumstances she had naturally gravitated towards Ryan. He wished he knew why.

A movement across the aisle, a sigh that was audible even above the whine of the twin Rolls-Royce engines, the closing of a file, and Ryan turned to find himself looking directly into the President's eyes. Kearney's mouth twisted, and the look he shot in Ryan's direction was a silent plea for understanding. Indeed, it was almost an apology.

Chad breathed out slowly and let his annoyance fade. He might as well berate the sun for shining or the rain for being wet; he had fallen in love with a man whose life was all hard choices, and it would be wrong to blame him for them. Over Berry's sleeping head, he signaled whatever it was Doug needed to see – forgiveness? acceptance? – and the reconciliation was effected without a word being uttered. Then the papers were stuffed back into the briefcase and Kearney detached his seat-belt and stepped across to take the rearward-facing seat opposite Chad. He leaned in towards him and their knees brushed lightly.

"I was right about you being a better father than I am. I can't remember the last time she did that with me."

Ryan's free hand reached out and patted one bony wrist.

"Maybe she thinks you're too important. You have to split yourself so many ways, and now I'm here as well that's one more share of you she doesn't get."

"She understands," said Kearney. "But you're right; I'm not superhuman, I can't be everywhere at once." He looked out of the window. "I love this country," he said, no arid political cliché but delivered from the heart. "I want to do the best I can for it, but it's determined to bleed me dry. This job takes everything you have, and then more, and then the rest; you don't expect to come out at the end of it with anything like the strength you had going in. I don't understand how anybody ever does two terms."

"And yet you're on the ballot for November?"

"Well, that's the problem. Presidents don't get to walk away, no matter how much we might like to. I'd have to be half-way to my grave before the Party would let me decline the nomination, and even then I'm not sure they'd be willing. I'm their servant, Chad, not their master."

"I know. I'm sorry."

"Me too. Deeply. And I'm really glad I've got you to share it with, but there are some things we're just not allowed to talk about – and what really happened in Kyrgyzstan is one of them. Can you stay around, knowing that I lied to you?"

"You didn't lie, you just didn't tell me everything you knew. I think the question should really be, do you still want me around knowing that sometimes I'm going to make mistakes?"

"I do," said Kearney, with the first trace of a smile he had managed for many hours. Then; "Actually I like how that sounds, don't you?"

"Hmmm," said Ryan. "I do, too."

And Berry, snuggled against his neck, lifted her sleepy head and said plainly; "So do I."

It was midnight before they crept in under the Portico and clambered wearily out of the car. Berry had revived somewhat on the run from Andrews, but still leaned against Ryan with her eyes hollow and fixed. Beyond her, Kearney slumped into the soft leather seat of the limousine, taciturn and exhausted, looking thirty years older than his age. Outside the windows, the city wore its lights like jewelry, arrayed layer by layer in strands of diamond and ruby finery; within was silence and acceptance and the burden of sour knowledge. If any of them had ever been mistaken enough to believe that great power could exist without great responsibility, they must have been disabused of the notion by now; fortunately not even Berry had entertained such a delusion, but perhaps not until this moment had any of them understood the enormity of the commitment Kearney had made – not only for his own sake but also for the sakes of those around him.

Kirsten was waiting as the motorcade drew to a halt. She stepped out of the bright hallway looking trim but fatigued, her hair caught in an unbecoming knot, her usual immaculate tailoring replaced by a raspberry pink tracksuit. It looked as if she had been trying to work out anxiety and jet-lag with an extended session of exercise, a determination that the two half-asleep men could hardly help admiring.

"Berry, sweetheart, you must be exhausted."

"I'm fine, mom; I slept on the plane." But the hug was tighter than usual and perhaps a little more heartfelt.

"You did? Good. Doug, are you okay?" Kirsten disentangled an arm from Berry to wrap it around her husband's neck and kiss his cheek.

"Short of sleep," he murmured, ruefully. "What else is new?"

"True." Kirsten turned her attention to Ryan. "How about you, buddy?"

"Tired," he admitted, accepting her extended hand and squeezing gently.

She smiled. "I'm glad to see everyone back safely; I missed you all. There's so much we need to talk about, but it can wait for now. Let's see if we can get some rest, shall we?"

"Sounds good," Ryan responded. Kearney merely grunted agreement. Berry did not speak.

Together, in a wan little crowd, surrounded by equally weary aides and agents, they bundled along the corridor, an uncoordinated rabble falling tiredly into the elevator and being whisked to the shelter of the Residence. As they stepped out into the quiet hall and Ryan's footsteps turned away from the group, Kirsten stopped him with a word.

"Goodnight," she said, gently. "Thank you for looking after my family."

His fair eyebrows rose. "I did nothing," he told her, mystified.

Kirsten, however, begged to differ. "You did everything," she assured him, with a heavy-eyed smile. "Sleep well, Chad."

"And you," he replied, softly. "All of you. Goodnight."

But he did not sleep well. It was a night of fragmentary dreams, of images that did not connect, of being in bed and switching off his higher functions without obtaining anything that warranted the name of rest. Five hours was enough; it was as graphic an exercise in futility as could ever have been imagined. Eventually Ryan accepted the inevitable, crawled into the shower, found clean clothes, and headed off to his custard-box of an office in the hopes of producing work that would justify his continued existence. Just at the moment he did not see the point of himself, but if he could accomplish some make-work task he should at least end up being able to cut himself a little more slack.

Fortunately, there were always tedious jobs to be done, reports to be read and initialed, questionnaires to be answered, stored voice-mails to be listened to and to which there would have to be responses. He made notes in his tidy handwriting, pausing to sip from time to time the creamy coffee he had obtained from the staff Mess, and had barely lifted his eyes from his papers for an hour or more when he became aware of a quiet commotion outside and a presence in his doorway.

"May I interrupt?" asked Kirsten. "I brought breakfast."

"Breakfast?" He was on his feet, greeting her automatically. "Please." He indicated his pathetic excuse for a so-called spare chair.

Kirsten placed a box on the table. "Apricot danish?" she offered.

"Thank you." And they sat, face to face in the little room, eating in companionable silence, while Kirsten's agent closed the door and discreetly stationed himself outside.

"Where's Doug?" he asked, between mouthfuls.

"In the Oval. He probably started work round about the same time you did this morning. I'm not surprised neither of you got much sleep." Then, forestalling the next question, she continued. "Berry hasn't surfaced yet. I don't think she really understood what happened yesterday and I wanted to thank you all for keeping her out of it. She really trusts you, Chad. She wants you to stay."

"I know." He was looking directly at her over the desk, over the small mountain of paperwork he was trying to shift from one pile to another in his maddeningly meticulous way. "I want that, too."

"Good. Then we all want the same." Kirsten was smiling. "Tell me, what did you think of the Lowman House?"

Ryan settled into his chair, took a breath, and thought a moment before replying. "I know you don't like the place, and I hate to disagree with you ... "

"But you adored it?"

"Yes."

Kirsten laughed, the freest and easiest sound he had heard in what seemed half a lifetime. "How did I guess?" she asked, rhetorically.

"Predictable much?" He almost felt like apologizing for it.

"Not really. Unless you count wanting to be wherever Doug wants to be. Which is good from my point of view, believe me, because there are going to be times in the next few years when he's going to need a wife to look after him and a lot of those times it won't be able to be me. From where I'm standing, you look as if you'd be willing to take on the job."

"Maybe," he admitted, smiling.

"Figure we can work out how to share him?"

Perhaps he should have expected the question, but he had not. He had thought that everything would be allowed to slide into some miasma of good-natured vagueness where the precise nature of their relationship would simply not be discussed. Kirsten's practical approach, however, was infinitely reassuring.

"Yes," he said, without equivocation. "I love him, you love him. I'm not seeing any conflict there."

"Neither am I. And you'll take him for better or worse, won't you, just the way I did?"

"Given the opportunity, I would do it exactly the way you did it."

"Good. That's what I thought." Kirsten brushed danish crumbs from her fingers and dabbed her mouth with the napkin from the box. "You need to know," she added, "that this latest business has shaken the hell out of Doug's confidence. I'm not going to discuss it in detail because I don't think either of us should know as much about it as we do, but it's undermined his faith in the people around him. In Howard, Brent McArdle, even in Mitch. We've known Mitch forever, but it never occurred to either of us that he could do anything like this. I don't know whether to admire or fear him for the strength of his principles."

"I guess," he said slowly, "we can do both."

"We probably don't have a choice," the First Lady concurred. "Doug's feeling the same way. He's wondering if he really wants to commit himself to another four years with these people. Not that he can back out of the election at this stage," she admitted, with a twist of her mouth, "but he could probably manage to throw the campaign somehow, if he wanted to."

"Do you think he will?"

"I don't know. I don't think he does yet, either. Don't try to discuss it with him, for God's sake; he's confused enough. Let's you and me just concentrate on making sure he feels good about his decision, shall we, whatever it is?"

"Like the good, supportive wives we both are?"

"Exactly." Kirsten crumpled the napkin and lobbed it inaccurately towards the waste-paper basket. It hit the lip and bobbled out, and she got to her feet to retrieve it and place it in the receptacle. "I have good news as well," she added, leaning over the desk and grinning at him conspiratorially. "It seems that Howard has withdrawn his objections to the private use of the pool. In fact, if you feel like going down to the basement at about eleven o'clock this morning, you could well find Doug there ahead of you."

"Thank you."

"You're welcome. I'm glad you're here, Chad. Doug's not an easy man to live with, but you and I both know that he's well worth the effort. I'll be very glad to have someone around to help me carry the load for a while."

"I'll do what I can," he promised, as she turned away. "Kirsten?"

"Yes?"

"The ghost. At the Lowman House." And if he felt even remotely stupid introducing the subject he was instantly reassured by the expression on her face, a compound of compassion and delight. "It isn't Gran'pa Herbert, is it?"

"Ah. No. I wondered if you'd realize. Have you worked out who it is?"

"I think so." For a moment he glanced down at his fingertips, almost as if he might find the answer there. Then he looked back up at her, gathered his courage, and said quietly; "It's Doug, isn't it?"

"Yes, it is. And there's nothing we can do to stop him haunting the place, Chad, so we definitely shouldn't try – but I think between us you and I have what it takes to prevent him ending up a miserable ghost. Do you believe you have the power to make him happy?"

"I know I do," he said. He had never been more certain of anything in his life.

"Yes," came the compassionate response. "I know it, too."

Late that morning Ryan found his way down to the basement. Joel, who was outside the door, admitted him with a world-weary smile; there was no discarded clothing in the changing-room, however, and no towels in evidence, only shoes and socks abandoned at the end of the bench. Chad kicked off his own footwear and stepped into the pool room, where the lighting was bright and the sound of fans and other equipment was no longer merely a background hum but had ripened into a bustling undertone.

Kearney was sitting on the edge, trousers rolled to his knees, feet dangling in the water. A silver coffee-tray with two cups lurked close to his elbow.

"Did you sleep at all?" was his first question.

"Some," Ryan acknowledged, rolling up his trousers and joining him. Without preliminary, Kearney poured him coffee and handed it over. "What's happening with Holofernes this morning?"

"Nothing surprising. Miraculously a group of about a hundred and fifty elite technicians managed to escape somehow, and equally miraculously there appears to have been a decontamination train in precisely the right place to pick them up. They'll be aboard that thing for weeks, but at least they're still alive. Got to hand it to the Chinese when it comes to contingency planning. Mind you," added Kearney – even more cynically, if such a thing were possible – "we're not too shabby in that department ourselves. We can 'contingency' with the best."

"You're thinking about Barrington."

"Yes. You realize you and I are going to have to talk about him some time?"

"That's why I'm here." Ryan sipped thoughtfully and looked at him over the lip of his coffee cup. "You didn't know in advance, did you? About his death?"

"Of course not. Not in detail. But there's an emergency order … " He paused. "Like Brent said, it's all about checks and balances. It has to be possible to take out any top government official if it becomes necessary. It's just that … " For a moment the President seemed to struggle, his fingers tangling together in a graphic display of unresolve. "You just never think it's going to be the guy you had breakfast with. I had no reason not to trust George – like I have no reason not to trust Brent, or you, or Kirsten – but now that I've seen the evidence, I'm fully convinced it was the right decision."

"Are you allowed to tell me … ?"

"What the evidence was? Some of it. Remember that dinner I went to at the Chinese Embassy back in May?"

"Sure."

"Well, George was there with me. That evening, apparently, he was set up with a new Chinese handler – quite a glamorous one, too, I understand – and he's been under constant surveillance ever since."

"Is that really all it takes to turn a man like that?" asked Ryan incredulously. "A honey trap? Isn't that the oldest trick in the book?"

"It is," replied Kearney, heavily, "but believe me, it was a hell of a lot more complicated in this case. George had a higher loyalty. I almost admire him for it, in a twisted kind of way."

"Higher than his loyalty to the country?"

"Much. His father, Sergeant Robert Eugene Barrington, went MIA in Korea in March 1953. Somehow the Chinese had managed to convince George that the old man was alive and that they could have him released in exchange for the right kind of information. You don't bribe someone like George with sex or money, Chad, but family … We're all vulnerable there."

Ryan was shaking his head in disbelief. "You're saying he alerted Beijing about the sabotage of Holofernes because he thought that somehow it would help him get his father back?"

"Basically, yes. Our end of the operation had been in place for years – before I took office, in fact – but we were waiting until the Chinese were ready to commission the plant, to achieve the maximum possible disruption. It was a belt and braces set-up; there may have been more than two sabotage teams for all I know, but one pair – the agents whose deaths we learned about on the night of the nuclear dinner – were working as volunteers with a French pollution-monitoring NGO. George was told about them, I was told about the train crew. It had to be something on that kind of scale in order to get the traitor to break cover, whoever he was."

"But whichever way it went down we would still have been ordering the deaths of our own guys?"

"That was inevitable. You never really believe in fanaticism until you realize there's somebody willing – eager, in fact – to drive a freight train full of Semtex into an underground facility and push the button. They signed up for it, Chad. Think about the kind of nerve it must have taken to do something like that."

"I can't," Ryan admitted, stunned. "I've tried, but it's more than I can process. But people do that kind of thing all the time, don't they? They use their deaths to give their lives some sort of meaning?"

"They do. And nine times out of ten nobody ever gets to hear about it and their names are forgotten. Which is exactly what would have happened to you if Captain Corrado had been a better shot, so don't pretend to me that you don't understand anything about sacrifice."

"That was different. It was spur-of-the-moment. I didn't have years to think about it."

"True. But if you had, wouldn't you still have done precisely the same?"

Ryan looked away. "I hope I would," he admitted at last. After this he was silent for an extended period but eventually he spoke again, calmly. "So, how did they decide it wasn't you? If you once start thinking your President might be a traitor, how do you go about proving to yourself that he isn't?"

Kearney groaned. "Now there," he admitted, "I also have you to thank. George was flitting backwards and forwards to see his Chinese handler, but the only new person I was seeing – or handling, for that matter – on a regular basis was you. And I'm sorry to say that I don't think there's a word you and I have said to each other since you walked into this house that hasn't been overheard and recorded. Embarrassing as that may be in retrospect, at least it was innocent in national security terms. When they finally concluded you were above suspicion, obviously it followed that I was, too. You gave me an alibi. Several, in fact."

"Wait, so Mitch ... and McArdle ... "

" ... and the Vice President, listened to us when we were together? Yes. Heard everything? Absolutely. And if you're wondering what that elaborate charade with the fake resignation was all about, I can only imagine that Howard and Mike Bennett cooked it up between them with the intention of shocking the living crap out of me. One way or another, at least it made me think about what I wanted for the future, which may not be completely in agreement with whatever it is they think I ought to want. But anyway, as a result they decided you and I were just what we said we were and we probably weren't planning to overthrow the Government any time soon. Which is kind of reassuring, given what happened to George."

"Meaning what?"

"Think about it, Chad. They had a fully-formed assassination plan ready and waiting for him the moment they needed it."

"You're telling me you think there was one ready for you, too?" He shook his head. "'*Will no-one rid me of this turbulent priest?*'" Never before had Henry II's disastrous invective against his troublesome archbishop seemed quite so apposite in a modern setting. "You walk a very fine line, Doug, don't you?"

"You'd better believe it. From what I've been told there's always a plan in place to assassinate a President of the United States; dates, locations and personnel may vary, but if the country needs to execute the boss in a hurry they're not going to want to waste time haggling over the details."

Ryan looked at him, appalled. "Have you any idea … ?"

"No, thank God, and I wouldn't want to, although crashing an executive jet into the middle of Lake Champlain would probably have a chance of succeeding. If Mitch and Brent hadn't decided to fly back with us last night, I might have been a little worried about our chances of getting home safely."

"But that would mean … Berry? The agents?"

"Berry," repeated Kearney. "The agents. You too. You'd have been collateral damage. But we lived, Chad, all of us, to fight another day."

"You're saying that after going to all that trouble, keeping Berry out of the way so that she wouldn't overhear anything … ?"

"They'd have let her die along with the rest of us? No doubt at all about it. I don't suppose it would have been McArdle's first choice, but he's a ruthless and dedicated man and you've got to break the eggs to make the omelette. We're all hostages to fortune, Chad. I just want to survive with my life intact – and the lives of the people I care about. This job is about as safe as going for a stroll in a minefield."

"Hmmm. Mitch warned me when I started working here; he said

everybody who got close to you had enemies. I thought he meant the Vice President but he didn't, did he?"

Kearney laughed, a raw, painful sound. "He probably, did but like him or hate him Howard's our guy all the way. No, it's not the enemy you can see that you need to worry about. You're a military man, you should know that as well as I do."

"I'm no tactician," came the quiet protest. "I never had to fight. I spent my working days designing and operating imaging systems."

"I've never fought anyone in earnest either, but it's pretty much the same with fires. You think you've got them under control but they burn around behind you, in the wall paneling or above the ceiling – and the next thing you know, there's no way out."

"Better the devil you know than the devil you don't?" whispered Ryan.

"Better by far," was the assurance. "You can deal with the devil you know."

"Yeah." And in the silence that fell, the quiet susurration of the pool water became the clamor of a full orchestra.

"We killed two birds with one stone when we destroyed Holofernes," continued Kearney. "We killed over a thousand birds, if it comes to that."

"Nobody gets the benefit of the doubt any more, do they?"

"That's right. We can't afford it."

But the tone in Kearney's voice was colder than it had been, and suddenly he was no longer talking about a threat that had been averted but about one that was still real and ever-present, and had only been temporarily postponed.

"Doug? What exactly did they have down there? It can't have been just warheads, it must have been something more. Something ... worse?"

"I can't tell you. And I'm not sure I'd want to, even if I could; I'd like you to be able to sleep at nights. This time we stopped them before they could deploy it, but believe me, Chad, they'll start up again more or less immediately. If they haven't already, of course. The price of freedom is eternal vigilance."

"It's just one great big global game of chess, isn't it? They move, we move. Armies, weapons, fortifications, we push them around the world in response to one another without ever considering that there are people attached. There's a line from a poem – about a checkerboard?"

The words came with an alacrity suggesting that they were never far from Kearney's mind.

" *'Tis all a Checkerboard of Nights and Days*
Where Destiny with Men for Pieces plays:
Hither and thither moves, and mates, and slays,
And one by one back in the Closet lays'."

"That's it," acknowledged Ryan. "A game of chess, with live pawns."

"I won't pretend there aren't consequences," was the rejoinder. "You don't reshape a thing without damaging it first. But if you imagine I didn't think about those guys, Chad, every single one of them, you're very much mistaken. I wouldn't want it not to be a struggle and neither would you; I wouldn't want to just flip a switch and have people stop existing. The people who died in Holofernes had families; they went to school, they had friends and first crushes and zits and were afraid of the dark. Every life has a story. Every story leaves a ghost."

"Even George?"

"Especially George. He's going to be haunting me for the rest of my life. The man was my friend, or I thought he was. I don't want to start distrusting people by default but when somebody you rely on for your own safety and that of the country turns out to be working for the enemy – and not even out of idealism but because he just can't let go of something in his own past – it makes you wonder if you're ever going to be able to depend on anyone else again. And then," he continued, his mood softening, "you realize that the person you've known for ten minutes means more to you than the one you've been working with for ten years, and that if the world's inevitably going to come crashing down around your ears he's the one you want to have beside you when it does."

"Thank you."

"Some things are just right, honey. You and me, we're right. We're going to go on being right, whatever happens."

"I know." A steadying hand landed on the President's shoulder, but instead of closing in to kiss him Ryan used the leverage to push himself to his feet. He pulled his shirt off over his head, shucked out of his jeans and underwear in a single movement, stood poised on the edge of the pool utterly naked in the dazzling glare of the lights.

"What?" asked Kearney, in confusion.

"Misuse of Government facilities. Even if everybody knows exactly what we're doing down here, it doesn't make me want to stop doing it. I don't care any more, Doug. What's the worst that can happen?" A moment later, he was in the water.

"Re-election," grumbled Kearney, scrambling upright and following suit.

They found each other somewhere out in the middle of the pool, in a confusion of wet arms and legs, amidst brightness and shouting echoes, sliding together with no attempt at concealment and almost in defiance of anyone who might eavesdrop on their privacy, their mouths hungry and their limbs and bodies tangling in a way that was becoming not so much familiar as absolutely essential.

"I'm going to have to stand up at that bastard's funeral and lie through my teeth," Kearney groaned, kissing his way down Ryan's neck and across his collarbone, and the juxtaposition of love and politics no longer seemed even remotely strange. "I'm going to have to say what a great guy he was and how much this country will miss him, and all the time he was threatening the people I love. I am the world's highest-paid hypocrite."

"The people you love?" Somehow Ryan had managed not to make any connection between Barrington and a direct threat to anyone in Kearney's immediate circle. The danger he had posed had been universal rather than personal, or so he had believed.

"Yesterday," came the explanation. "We had breakfast together yesterday. If it hadn't been for McArdle suggesting that the French could be involved in the destruction of Holofernes, George would probably have realized that we knew all about him. And if he hadn't felt that he was safe ... "

"He was in the house," said Ryan, quietly. "He could have killed us all."

"I doubt it. The Secret Service are pretty good. But there's no denying he could have done a lot of damage before they stopped him."

"He did," reflected Ryan. "He did a lot of damage."

"Yes. And I'm selfish enough to be grateful that he didn't do a whole lot more."

Ryan lay easy in his arms, buoyed by the water, feeling some of the recent wounds beginning to heal, wondering if there could be a future for them after all.

"Do you think he genuinely believed his father could still be alive in North Korea even after all these years?" he asked, after a while.

"Why not?" rumbled Kearney, close to his ear. "We're expected to believe the impossible all the time; according to the laws of aerodynamics a bumblebee shouldn't be able to fly, but we see it happening and so we believe it. People take on trust all sorts of things they can never explain and that can't logically be true, like Berry and her ghosts."

"So Barrington thought that if he just wished hard enough for his father to be alive it would happen, quite spontaneously and totally against logic?"

"It's called faith," said Kearney. "We use it to move mountains."

"It's awesome. I can't imagine ever believing in anything that much."

"Oh, come on, I bet you do. I bet there's at least one thing in your life you believe in that would make the rational world think you were completely insane. Isn't there anything that you cling to relentlessly, no matter how little sense it makes to anybody else?"

Ryan thought about it for a moment. "You," he said at last. "I believe in you. It makes no sense that we're together, but we are. Like we made it happen just by wanting it to. Like mind over matter."

"Yes. Like the bumblebee. Like George's father. There doesn't have to be a logical explanation."

"Just as well," smiled Ryan. "Because there isn't one. It just is."

"Uh-huh. Well, it probably won't surprise you to learn, honey, that in this case I'm exceptionally glad it 'is'. I'm quite prepared to take every little bit of it on trust."

Ryan turned in his arms, bringing their mouths together, luxuriating in the strength that held him and, just for this while, in the peace and isolation of their private place in the world.

"To tell you the truth, Mr President," he said, in a tone of utter contentment, "I'd have to admit that I am, too."

References

The toad beneath the harrow knows exactly where each tooth-point goes
Rudyard Kipling: *Paget M.P.*

A man of sorrows, and acquainted with grief
Isaiah Chapter 53 Verse 3

Tis all a Checkerboard of Nights and Days …
Edward Fitzgerald: *The Rubáiyát of Omar Khayyám*

About Adam Fitzroy

Imaginist and purveyor of tall tales Adam Fitzroy is a UK resident who has been successfully spinning male-male romances either part-time or full-time since the 1980s, and has a particular interest in examining the conflicting demands of love and duty.

Made in the USA
Charleston, SC
25 March 2015